The Ballerino and the Biker

REBECCA JAMES

BOOK ONE OF THE HEDONIST SERIES

THE BALLERINO AND THE BIKER
COPYRIGHT © 2018 BY REBECCA JAMES

ISBN 978-1-98042-227-3

COVER CONTENT IS FOR ILLUSTRATIVE PURPOSES ONLY. ANY PERSON DEPICTED
ON THE COVER IS A MODEL

COVER ARTIST REESE DANTE

EDITED BY JENNI LEA AT PROOF YOUR LOVE, BETA READ BY JILL WEXLER

SPECIAL THANKS TO JENNI LEA AT PROOF YOUR LOVE FOR EDITING, AND TO THE
TALENTED REESE DANTE FOR THE INCREDIBLE COVER.

WARNING: THIS BOOK CONTAINS A SCENE OF MILD ASSAULT AND BATTERY.

CHAPTER ONE

Morgan

My neck and shoulders hurt, and my hip was making that clicking sound again, but that was standard fare for me. What threatened to undo me was the colossal crack in my emotional armor as I stared at the freshly covered grave of my only brother. Jake and I hadn't been close, but we were getting there. Now we never would.

Nikki touched my shoulder.

"You ready to go?" she asked, wrapping her arms around my waist and squeezing fiercely. She was family to me. Now the only family I had.

I hugged her briefly in return before shaking my head.

"I know you've got to get to work. I need some time alone anyway." I kissed the top of her head. "Thanks for coming."

She poked me with a long fingernail hard enough to make me yelp. "Why are you thanking me? You know I wanted to be here."

I rubbed my chest. "God, you're a bitch."

She winked at me, and I watched her trudge toward her car before bending and picking up one of the white roses from the top of the coffin. I walked up hill to where my parents were buried, a chill running down my back as I got close to the elaborate Wentworth headstone. The cold, dark slate and boldly etched lettering ominously reminded me I was the only Wentworth left, completely and utterly alone. No parents, no brother, no distant relatives. Just me, Morgan Alexander Wentworth.

After two years, my parents' graves still showed the seams of burial. I tossed the rose under their names, memories creeping from the recesses of my mind.

THE BALLERINO AND THE BIKER

I'd just performed a perfect series of pirouettes to the praise of Arturo, my most difficult-to-please instructor, when an academy administrator had appeared, taking me to his office to break the news that both my parents had been killed in an automobile accident. The next thing I'd known, I'd been hustled onto a flight to the States.

I'd received curious looks from people at the funeral who'd expected me to be devastated, but my parents had been emotionally distant, and I'd become accustomed to being away from them. I'd felt closer to most of my dance instructors.

I'd become an orphan at sixteen, as well as the CEO of a large corporation, and all I'd been able to think was I couldn't wait to get back to Milan and dance. I'd given little thought to that day since then, but as I stood shifting from one foot to the other on the well-manicured cemetery lawn, it all vividly came back to me.

The funeral had been long, but the burial blessedly short. When the crowd had dispersed, some pausing to pat me on the back or kiss my cheek before heading for their cars, I'd thought to escape to the limousine waiting to take me to my parents' penthouse. But the president of Wentworth Properties had cornered me before I could.

After a smooth delivery of condolences, Gerald Peters had asked what my plans were.

"I need to go back to Milan," I'd answered uncertainly. "I have two more years of study there."

"And Wentworth Properties?" Gerald had asked.

I'd frowned, unsure of what he was getting at. "You can run the company while I'm away, can't you?"

"Morgan, I know your father had always hoped you'd want to run Wentworth Properties one day, but we both know he didn't foresee dying before you could be properly groomed for the position. And let's face it; ballet is your heart and soul. Now, the shareholders have discussed it, and we'd like to buy you out."

I'd stiffened, mixed feelings warring in my breast. Although well-aware that selling my shares would make everything much easier for me, the company was mine, and I'd known I couldn't relinquish it so easily.

"I have to think about it," I'd told Peters, and the frustration and annoyance had been plain on his face.

After leaving the cemetery, I'd had my lawyer call a meeting, at which the board had tried to convince me to take two million dollars and ten percent equity in the company for my fifty-one shares in my family's twenty-million-dollar business. It had been obvious by the looks on the board members' faces, most of them old friends of my father's who had received loyalty shares after helping to get the company started, none had known Harvey Franks, my father's good friend and attorney, had been appointed my legal guardian. After telling them their offer was inadequate and that I was not ready to let go of my shares at that time, Harvey had drawn up papers giving Peters the title of President and COO, but leaving me in ultimate control of Wentworth Properties. Harvey would sit on the board in my stead while I finished my studies in Milan.

The board members hadn't looked happy, and many had cast frustrated and annoyed looks at Peters, as though the man had gone back on a promise. I hadn't cared. I knew Peters would run the company well, and that if he didn't, Harvey would let me know about it. I would hang on to my legacy until I was better able to make an informed decision, and in the meantime, I was free to return to the dance academy in Milan.

Crazy to think just two and a half years later, I stood in the same graveyard, staring at the same tombstone. This time, real grief and regret consumed me rather than the numb indifference I'd felt that day. My brother had left home when I was still a child. Jake hadn't known how to get in touch with me until after our parents' deaths. We'd begun to talk long distance and had agreed when I graduated from the academy and returned to New York City, we'd take the time to really get to know each other.

Well, I was back, but that would never happen.

I'd seen Jake at our parents' funeral, standing on the far hill with his motorcycle club surrounding him. From a distance, he'd looked so much like Dad, I'd immediately recognized him. Like our father, Jake was tall, broad, and powerfully built. I had the willowy frame of my mother, better suited to the art form I'd fallen in love with.

A part of me had hoped Jake would approach that day, but the saner portion had known he wouldn't. Everyone there had been aware my parents had disowned their oldest son, the "black sheep" of the Wentworth family. And Jake's biker buddies would have stuck out like sore thumbs among my parents' elite friends, neighbors, and business acquaintances.

I'd felt like an outsider, not belonging with the guests at the funeral nor with Jake and his club, and intensely jealous of the latter. I'd wanted the brother I'd been denied, but our mother and father had continued to stand between us, even after death.

A warm breeze blew over me, tousling my hair. This was August, not January, and Jake wasn't standing on the hill watching. He lay yards away, buried beneath six feet of dirt. I retraced my steps to his grave. A huge spray of red and yellow roses—club colors— stood at the head of the freshly turned earth beside the white lilies Nikki had brought and the roses I'd ordered for the coffin. Nikki and I had been the only ones there to say goodbye to my brother.

Anger churned in my gut.

Jake deserved more than two people at his god-damned funeral.

"Where the fuck is your precious club now?" I said aloud to the still summer air before turning to make my way to the car.

CßÐ

I slammed the door of my father's BMW, nose crinkling with distaste. The car had been sitting in a garage for two years, yet it still smelled of his expensive cigars. I should sell it. I really didn't need a car in the city where it was easier to walk twelve blocks than to find a parking space. I hated cabs and Ubers, unable to relax in the presence of a driver. Nikki called me ridiculous, but I think it stemmed from the disengaged manner in which my parents had treated their personal driver and how much it had bothered me as a child.

Searching my phone's music list, I chose Felix Mendelssohn's score for *A Midsummer Night's Dream* and pulled out of the cemetery parking lot.

Nikki and I had been together at the Global School of Ballet for four years before my parents had abruptly transferred me to their Milan academy, stating I'd be better off there. She'd flown to visit me several times over the years, and I was thankful to have her to return to now that I was home again.

The day the Manhattan Ballet Master-in-Chief had called to tell me he'd been following my progress and was inviting me to apprentice with the ballet company, I'd immediately called Nikki. She'd been over the moon for me.

Although from a well-off family, Nikki worked and paid for her own place. As I wasn't anxious to kick Gerald Peters out of the penthouse I'd been renting to him since my parents' deaths, both because I didn't want the confrontation and I didn't want to live there, I was staying with Nikki until I could move into the dorms at the school.

I turned onto East 6th Street, the trip from the cemetery having passed on autopilot. I pulled the BMW into the underground garage, parked in one of the two spaces reserved for Nikki, and climbed out of the car.

The elevator was broken, and I had to take the stairs. As I climbed, I determinedly left behind the dour feelings of the morning and concentrated on what needed to be done. I would be moving into the residence hall in a little over a week, and having entered the apprenticeship nearly three months late, I barely had time to prepare. As I unlocked Nikki's apartment door with the spare key she'd given me, I mentally ticked off my to-do list: *Wash my mountain of dirty laundry. Shop for sheets and incidentals. Order at least three pairs of tights.*

Two steps inside the apartment, I was kicking away my gray slacks while peeling off the black silk shirt I'd chosen that morning. As always, anything but a T-shirt, tights, and a dance belt felt wrong on my body. Walking around in my underwear was the next best thing.

I stretched and scratched my stomach. I knew Nikki wouldn't be back from the bookstore where she worked until after five. Maybe we could eat dinner together if she didn't have plans with her boyfriend, but I needed something in my stomach now. I grabbed a dwarf banana from the bowl on the ledge between the small kitchen and living room and ate it while admiring Nikki's framed posters of Ivan Vasiliev and Roberto Bolle. The lines of the dancers' bodies in movement never failed to fascinate me, even more so now that I'd realized my own body looked much the same when I danced. Years of intense practice had paid off. I wondered if I could get an hour of practice in before starting on all the things I needed to do.

Someone cleared their throat behind me, and I froze, banana to my lips. Nikki's boyfriend Paul worked with her. I knew he was at the bookstore now. No one else had a key to this apartment. I swung around and threw the banana as hard as I could directly into the intruder's face before darting for the door.

"Ow! What the fuck?"

Before I could reach the small foyer, what felt like two tons of steel muscle barreled into me, slamming me against the wall, a vise-like grip holding my wrists above my head. I opened my mouth to yell and fingers clapped over it, the scent of cigarettes sharp in my nose. The man's heart beating against my own felt strangely intimate in such a terrifying moment. I struggled to raise my knee, but his grip was too tight.

"Calm down," a low voice growled into my ear.

When the hand over my mouth loosened, I rasped out, "What do you want?"

"I'm taking you with me," the man said, and I panicked, struggling with everything I had. I was in excellent shape, but the man was a fucking powerhouse, several inches taller and about forty pounds heavier than I was. By the feel of him, those forty pounds were all muscle. What did he want with me? He was going to be mighty pissed if he anticipated a ransom, as there wasn't a Wentworth left to pay it, although I supposed he could call Peters. *Ha, as if that asshole would pay a dime for my life. He'd probably pay the guy to keep me.*

"There's a couple hundred dollars and an ATM card in my wallet. Take it and go," I blurted when I realized I couldn't get away.

"I don't want your money, kid."

What the fuck did he want, then? I suddenly became aware of a hardening length pressed against my lower back, and my heart went into over-drive. I took a breath to yell again, and the intruder's hand clapped down hard. This time I managed to get part of his finger between my teeth.

"Fuck!" The thug jerked his hand away, grabbed me by the back of the neck, and shoved me toward the bedroom. "Get dressed and pack a bag. I don't have time to wrestle with some goody two-shoes ballerina!"

I stalled between him and the bedroom, rubbing my hands over my suddenly cold arms.

"The term is *ballerino*, at least in Italy. How did you know I'm a dancer?"

My scary captor let out a huff. "I'm one of the fucking psychic twins." He pointed at my half-open duffel stuffed with dance gear. "You're bag's right there, genius. Now get moving."

He followed me into Nikki's bedroom. I tried not to look as terrified as I felt, no mean feat when wearing only a pair of black Calvin Kleins. As I gathered some clothes, I darted glances at the man watching me. Muscles in his arms bunched where he crossed them over his barrel of a chest, multiple tattoos interrupted tan skin, a white bent bar piercing decorated his right brow, and a ball in his tongue that he kept scraping against his teeth. He had blond hair and a close beard, and brilliant blue eyes blazing with animosity. All of which painted a picture of a fierce street thug, albeit a hot one. He looked slightly familiar.

"Who are you, and what do you want with me?" I asked. I wished my voice hadn't wavered with fear.

"Name's Zeke, and I want you to get your ass in gear. Now, hurry it up."

Zeke.

His cell phone vibrated, and he dug into his pocket for it. I took advantage of the moment to dart past him, running for the door. If I could reach the hall, maybe one of the neighbors —

Zeke caught my arm as I reached the edge of the living room. When I almost succeeded in wiggling away, he lunged into what became a full-body slam to the hardwood floor, sending shooting pains into my hip bones. There were going to be bruises if I lived long enough for them to form.

I struggled in Zeke's grip, his hot breath wafting over the side of my face. His hands tightened around my biceps. "Stop wriggling, you little queer!"

Instinctively, I stilled, but my mind was racing. Was this a bashing? Had he seen me on the street and thought I was an easy target? But how the fuck had he gotten into Nikki's apartment? And why did he look familiar? Was he a neighbor? As my mind cleared, I registered something that belied his homophobic words. Or maybe they didn't; perverts didn't exactly make sense.

I pushed back with my pelvis so my ass cradled the long, thick, undeniably hard length of him. Predictably, he shot away from me. I flipped over, suddenly more angry than scared.

"Seems you enjoy being pressed against the little *queer*." I kicked out with my foot, landing squarely on Zeke's solar plexus, and relished the sound of the air going out of his lungs.

THE BALLERINO AND THE BIKER

Zeke's blue eyes watered as he struggled to take a breath, and my gaze raked over him more thoroughly, stopping at a tattoo on his upper arm of a devil's face with its tongue licking out of a grinning mouth. I recognized it. *Zeke was a member of Jake's motorcycle club.*

Before I could speak again, Zeke grabbed me and pulled my face close to his. "Cooperate, princess. I'm here to save your ass."

This time he easily avoided my foot.

I was furious. Jake's crew didn't see fit to attend his funeral, but one of them broke into Nikki's apartment to scare the fuck out of me?

For what seemed an eternity, we sat staring each other down before Zeke leaned in until our noses touched, pushing my elbows back to the floor. We were chest to chest, and I could feel the heat pouring off him.

Sudden arousal zipped through me as the biker's eyes narrowed to slits. "I said, cooperate. You're in a precarious position right now."

I knew hurting a brother's family would go against the club's principles, and, as scary as some of them looked, the Hedonists weren't unlawful; Jake had assured me of that. So, Zeke's little attempt at scaring me wasn't going to work.

Now I knew who he was, I was determined to get back at him. I smiled. "I'd say you're the one in the precarious position." I thrust up my hips and ground sleazily against Zeke's groin. He fell backward and struggled to his feet, chest heaving and eyes flashing. I was sure I saw more than anger there, and it amused me a tough guy like him could be so easily disarmed.

"Tell me why you want me to go with you," I demanded.

Zeke ran a hand through his blond hair.

"Like I said, I'm trying to help you. The mess your brother got himself into directly affects you."

I tilted my head to the side. "What mess? Come on, you don't expect me to let you haul me away on your bike without an explanation." Encouraged by his scowl, I fluttered my lashes. "Unless this is how you usually pick up a guy. If so, I should tell you, wining and dining tends to be more effective than kidnapping."

"Cut. It. Out." Towering over me, the biker looked even more impressive. The blue tank he wore barely covered his rippling physique, and his jeans looked like they were molded to him. I could clearly see the semi he sported through the denim.

"Gonna call me a queer again?" I asked.

Zeke took a deep breath and let it out. "Look, I didn't mean to say that. Would you just listen to me a minute? When Lips hit that tree, there was a girl on the back of his bike."

I'd forgotten my brother's club name was Lips. He hadn't been fond of it, as I recall. Zeke's words sank in.

"Wait, what? Someone was with Jake when he died?"

Suddenly cold, I pulled my thighs against my chest and propped my chin on my knees.

Zeke looked away and seemed to deflate a little. "Yeah. Look, we don't have all day, kid. Pack a bag."

I closed my eyes and rested my forehead on my knees for a moment. "I'm not moving until you explain why I need to go with you."

Zeke made an exasperated sound like I should know the answer to that.

"Spoons didn't take it so well your brother was with his girl."

I raised my head. "*Spoons?*"

"The guy's got a legit reason for being called that, and you don't wanna know what that is."

Of course, that just made me try to come up with why a member of an MC might be called *Spoons*. I stretched my legs out and crossed them at the ankles, leaning back on my elbows like I had all the time in the world and enjoying the way Zeke tensed all over. I had to admit, I got a perverse pleasure out of annoying him.

"Is it because he melts his drugs in a spoon before shooting up?" I asked.

Zeke gave me a long-suffering look before starting to pace. I tried again.

"Does he spoon out a guy's intestines if he won't give him what he wants?"

"Jesus Christ on a Harley! You've got a wild imagination, kid. You ain't gonna stop till you know, are you?" He stopped in front of me and sighed. "It's because of the way he quietly spoons a guy before sliding his blade into their gut."

"Oh." I was kind of disappointed. "That doesn't sound as scary as the guts thing."

Zeke looked like he was counting in his head. After a moment, he stuck out a hand to help me up. "Come on, brat. We gotta get outta here before the Steel Pistons figure out Lips had a little brother, and they start looking to retaliate."

"What?" I gripped his hand and let him pull me to my feet. Underneath the cigarettes, he smelled good. Like spice and... fire. *Man, that sounded lame.*

"All that Beethoven or whatever you dance to make you deaf or something? *Retaliate.* That means it's you Spoons'll be cozying up to with his blade next."

When I continued to stare up at him, Zeke's mouth flattened into a thin line, and he turned and walked into the bedroom. I could hear drawers opening and closing. He returned a moment later with a backpack stuffed full of the clothes I'd dropped earlier plus a few extras.

"Either you're staying here with a chick, or you like to dress like one."

"This is my friend Nikki's place."

"Thank God."

I frowned. "There's nothing wrong with a man dressing like a woman."

Zeke grunted and tossed the shirt I'd worn to the funeral my way. I stared at it as an odd numbness crawled over me.

"Come on, you gotta do some of the work," Zeke mumbled as he attempted to help me into it. The soft material settled at my waist, and I took a deep breath, bending to slowly pull my trousers up with Zeke gripping my arm to keep me steady.

"Guess you've had a pretty rough day," he said, and I had to agree. It all seemed to be catching up with me.

Zeke kicked my Italian loafers at me, and I slowly slipped my feet into them. My backpack on his shoulder, Zeke opened the door of my apartment and stuck his head out.

He looked back at me. "Coast is clear, princess. Come on."

Hesitating, I asked, "If this guy's really after me, shouldn't we go to the cops?"

Zeke's blue eyes met mine. "Hell, no. You think they'd listen? You're safest with us while we come up with a plan. So, unless you wanna wind up a lampshade in the Pistons' clubhouse, let's get a move on."

"Jesus. So much for my wild imagination." I grabbed my duffel of dance clothes and followed Zeke out.

10

CHAPTER TWO

Morgan

Being a back warmer to a hot guy on a Harley should be a sexy experience, but I was too busy clinging to Zeke like a monkey and hoping we wouldn't crash to fully appreciate it. When I'd refused to get on the bike without a helmet, Zeke had strapped his to my head and gone without. The bike vibrated between my thighs, its roar filling my ears and helping me to zone out as I pressed my cheek to Zeke's broad back and kept my eyes tightly shut.

When the bike came to a stop, I eased my rigid fingers from Zeke's rock-hard abs and leaned away from him, immediately missing the warmth of his body. The day was mild, but I still felt ice cold.

"Climb off," Zeke said.

Belatedly, I realized he couldn't dismount the bike until I did. Blushing, I did so and took a moment to look around the garage to cover my embarrassment. A car was parked in the middle, nose out with the hood propped open and a large toolbox nearby. I counted eight motorcycles lining the far wall.

"Wow, that's a lot of bikes," I said lamely.

Zeke gave me a look that said *no shit* as plainly as though he'd spoken the words and opened a door to the house. "After you." He stood back to let me pass with an exaggeratedly grand sweep of his arm before following me in.

Knowing my brother's club had been family to him didn't make it any easier for me to walk into that place. What I'd expected, I don't know—maybe a run-down meeting room or a grungy pool hall with skulls on the wall. Instead, I walked down a short hall and into what looked to be a regular living room, although there were a couple pool

11

tables off to the side and a painting of a half-naked woman on the wall. Zeke caught me staring at it.

"Tony dabbles in oils," he said in a snooty voice before laughing at his own joke.

I turned away, not really blaming him for being a jerk after I'd given him such a hard time back at Nikki's apartment. Two black leather couches faced a large-screen TV currently broadcasting a football game. I didn't follow sports, so I couldn't say what teams were playing. A hot-as-hell guy with long, dark-blond hair sat on one of the couches, arms resting on the back and jeans riding low on his narrow waist.

He looked me over, a smile spreading across his handsome face. "This's gotta be Morgan; he looks so much like Jake. Good work bringing him in, Zeke."

"You make me sound like a felon with an APB out on him," I said nervously.

Zeke sighed. "Morgan, this is Dante."

My name on the bikers' lips sounded weird, but I guess it made sense they all knew it because of Jake, and Zeke had only chosen to call me *princess* and *tiny dancer* because he was an ass. I shook Dante's hand.

"Zeke says I'm in some kind of danger," I said.

"You definitely are, babe," Dante said.

"You sure do look like your brother."

I turned to find a tall Latino man, older than Zeke and Dante, had walked into the room and stood to the side surveying me. "Same pretty mouth."

"That's why we called Jake *Lips*," Dante told me.

"Jake said it was because he mouthed off," I said.

They all laughed. "Yeah, he didn't appreciate the compliment," the Latino said. He extended a hand to me. "Hung."

"Excuse me?"

"My name," he clarified, a twinkle in his dark eyes.

I shook his hand. "Oh. You don't look Chinese."

Zeke and Dante broke into guffaws.

"That ain't why they call him Hung." Dante nudged me with a booted foot.

As realization dawned, a blush spread up my neck into my cheeks.

Hung winked. "Real name's Dick."

"You're kidding me."

Hung just grinned.

"Show Morgan to Lips's room," Dante said. "Blaze'll be here soon."

Blaze. "That's the club president, right? Jake's best friend?" I followed Zeke down the hall. We passed the kitchen where a couple of women stood at the stove chatting and laughing with a lithe young man who held a little white dog in his arms.

"Right. He's real torn up over Lips. He's the one who sent me to get you."

"Could you do me a favor and not refer to my brother as *Lips?* His name was Jake."

Zeke shrugged. "He was Lips to us. Except Blaze called him J."

We climbed a set of rickety stairs.

"Oh, yeah. And Jake called Blaze *B*, right?"

Zeke opened a door at the end of the hall. "Yeah. B and J."

Zeke's neck turned red. What was running through the biker's mind might as well have been a neon sign over his head. I decided to give him a break and didn't comment, sliding past him into the room.

I stopped. I hadn't anticipated the shock of seeing the place Jake had made all his video calls to me from, and it hit me like a ton of bricks.

"Something wrong, kid?" Zeke asked.

I shook my head and made my feet move farther into the room. A colorful quilt decorated the single bed and beige curtains covered the window. Posters of female models in bikinis, and motorcycles, and female models in bikinis on motorcycles hung on the walls. Sadness poured over me knowing this was where Jake had lived for so many years. Not that it was a bad place, but he should have been at home with us. Not that I'd stayed at home very long. Maybe our parents hadn't really wanted children.

Zeke set my bags on the chair by the desk and opened the curtains, sending dust motes floating about the room.

"How long do I need to stay here?" I asked, slumping resignedly onto the bed. I badly wanted to dance.

"No clue," Zeke said. "Blaze can fill you in."

I couldn't resist. "Is he a pyromaniac?"

Zeke frowned. "Huh?"

"*Blaze?* Does he like to start fires?"

The look on Zeke's face was worth having to hold back my laughter. "No. That's his real name, princess." He turned and left, shaking his head.

It felt good to smile. I lay for a while staring at one of the bikini models on the wall before rooting through my things for my cell phone and dialing Nikki's number.

"Hey, Morgs. Where'd you go? Thought you'd be home when I got here. The shop was dead, and Paul covered the rest of my shift."

I heard water and clanking sounds in the background and figured she must be making dinner.

"I'm with friends of Jake's."

The water turned off.

"What? You mean his club?"

"Yeah."

"Why?"

"It's complicated."

"Tell me."

I related everything I knew.

"You're saying this gang is going to be out to get you for something your brother did?"

"Evidently that's how things work in Thugs-ville," I said, picking at a string on the quilt.

"You must be upset. You're being snarky."

She knew me so well. "I'm fine."

"I don't like the sound of this."

"I'm sure it's just for a day or two. I'll call you when I know more."

A knock on the bedroom door had me saying goodbye. I tossed the phone on the bed and got up to find Dante standing in the hall. He smiled a wide, toothy smile that probably got all the girls' panties wet, and a few of the boys', too.

"Dinner's ready."

"Oh. Okay." I followed Dante through the kitchen into a dining room where about twenty big, brawny guys sat with several girls in shorts and tiny T-shirts. Everyone was laughing and talking as they passed steaming plates of food around until they spotted us and went quiet.

REBECCA JAMES

A familiar-looking man with jet black hair and blue eyes stood up from where he'd been seated at the head of the table. Was every guy in this club fucking gorgeous?

The man smiled. "Morgan, glad to have you with us. I'm Blaze, president of the Hedonists. Your brother was my best friend."

Suddenly shy due to all the stares, I stiffened a little and nodded my head at the guy. "Hi."

Blaze indicated the chair between him and Dante, and I sat down. I felt Zeke's eyes on me but didn't look at him.

"Eat, everyone. We'll have introductions after," Blaze said, and the group began talking and passing plates again.

I relaxed and filled my dish. Blaze turned to me, face solemn.

"I'm sorry about your brother. I miss him like hell. We all feel the loss. J loved you a lot... I hope you know that."

I looked away, nose stinging with the threat of tears.

Blaze squeezed my shoulder. "J made me promise if something happened to him, I'd find you and make sure you were all right. Considering who Jake had with him on his bike, I thought it'd be better if you stayed with us for a while. I would've come to get you myself, but I had to work. Zeke treat you okay?"

I glanced at Zeke.

"Yeah. Fine."

"Good."

"You knew about Jake seeing this rival guy's girl?" I asked Blaze.

"Hell, no. I would've done something about it, and he knew that. I'm sure it's why he kept it a secret. He was playing a deadly game, and he lost."

"He must have really cared about her," I said, wondering why Jake hadn't mentioned the girl to me. I was sure I'd asked him if he was dating anybody more than once.

"I'm sure he did, to do something that crazy." Blaze chewed a chunk of roasted potato. "Vanessa worked in the business, and so did Jake. I guess that's how they hooked up." He sighed. "Unfortunately, the Steel Pistons aren't gonna take this lying down. Afraid that's bad news for you, kiddo." Blaze kept his tone light, but a crease between his eyes showed his concern.

"I don't understand. When it comes right down to it, I hardly knew my brother," I said. "How can they think this is my fault?"

15

"It's all about retribution," Dante spoke from the other side of me.

Blaze nodded. "J took someone Spoons loved, so Spoons thinks he needs to take someone J loved in return, even though J isn't here to know it. We're here. An eye for an eye. Fortunately, he's not automatically gonna know about you since you haven't been around. If we're lucky, he won't find out, but we couldn't take that chance. We've gotta keep an eye on you until we know."

"It's the reason we weren't at the service," Dante said, answering the question that had been bothering me. "We had our own wake here at the clubhouse and burned J's leather in a bonfire. We made sure the Pistons knew about it, and we hoped it would keep 'em away from the funeral."

Fear scuttled up the back of my neck. I hadn't really thought it was that serious. Could this gang really think hurting me would make losing someone any easier? It was fucking crazy.

"Don't worry, kid," Hung said. "You'll be safe with us."

"I'm not a kid. I'm nineteen."

Chuckles from around the table had my hackles rising. I pushed away my plate and stood. "Look, I'm fine. Really. I'm staying with a friend."

"A chick," Zeke said.

Blaze got to his feet. "We can have someone watch you at your friend's, but you'd be doing me a favor if you stay a couple weeks until I can see what's going down. Just for a while, Morgan. Until the heat is off. I want to do this for J."

"But I'm starting an apprenticeship with the Manhattan Ballet. I'm supposed to move into student housing at the end of next week."

"We should know what's going on by then."

I shook my head. "I don't get it. Why do you care? I get it that Jake was like family to you—he told me that. But my brother's gone, and technically, you don't know me at all."

Blaze put a hand on my shoulder. "That's just how it works. Family is family, even by extension."

Not knowing what to say to that and afraid I might do something embarrassing like burst into frustrated tears, I turned and fled to the room they'd given me.

CR&O

For a day and a half, I made myself scarce, only coming out of my room to eat and to go to the bathroom. Using my playlist on my phone, I practiced as much as I could, losing myself in movements that almost came naturally to me after years of dance, but there was only so much I could do in the small space.

I met most of the club, but the only one I really talked to regularly was Dante, who made a point of knocking on my door every so often. Sometimes he only plopped onto the bed and watched me practice or sat scrolling through his phone. I became comfortable in his presence and found it amusing he looked more like a romance novel version of a biker than a real one — the kind who would stand shirtless beside his bike, long hair blowing in a hot wind and a menacing look on his chiseled face. It was weird how most of the club were a little too good-looking to be real. Like Blaze. And Zeke, my new shadow. He rarely spoke, but I could always feel his eyes on me.

The clubhouse was on a back street in Clinton Hill, a neighborhood I'd previously never ventured into because it wasn't considered to be the safest. Even though I'd known my brother was part of an MC, I'd never really imagined the kind of neighborhood that entailed.

There was a warehouse on the lot behind the clubhouse. Jake had told me they made films or something, which might have accounted for everyone's good looks. I didn't ask about it. Jake was gone, and I wasn't going to be there long, so what did it matter?

As far as I could tell, only a few members lived in the clubhouse full-time. The others came and went on their own schedules, sometimes eating together, watching TV, or playing pool. I'd seen more than one sacked out on the couch since I'd gotten there. I'd been given one of the three bedrooms, the other two being occupied by Blaze and Dante. Blaze had a steady girl who more often than not looked like she wanted to rip someone's head off, and all they seemed to do was fuck, the sound of the bed banging against the wall of Blaze's bedroom a regular backdrop when she was around.

I kept expecting Gerald Peters to call me, but my phone remained silent except for a daily check-in from Nikki, and I wasn't sure that was a good thing. I was back in the city for good, so shouldn't I become a little more involved? I needed to get to Wentworth Properties to see for myself what was going on. Up to that point, I'd been relying on Harvey's reports on monthly board meetings, but I made a mental note to let both Harvey and Peters know I would be going myself from then on. I'd work it out somehow. Hell, I was the CEO—they could arrange them around my dance schedule, I told myself, even though the thought of demanding such a thing felt weird.

The third morning of my stay, one of the guys walked into the kitchen while I was scrounging in the pantry for something to eat. The club called him Swish, and by the way he moved his hips when he walked, there was no need to ask why. He held a dog in his arms, but it wasn't the same one I'd seen a few nights ago when I saw him.

"Hey," Swish said. He crossed the kitchen and disappeared onto the screened-in porch, returning a moment later sans dog. He lit a cigarette and regarded me with dark, black-lined eyes.

"Hi." I'd chosen an individual box of bran cereal, undoubtedly a reject from a variety pack, and poured it into a bowl.

Swish was lean—almost gaunt—and flamboyant in a way that seemed put-on, like he was throwing his sexuality in everyone's face. He seemed, to me, an unlikely addition to an MC, particularly one with members like Zeke who threw derogatory words around, although he hadn't called me a queer again. I didn't recall Swish being in the picture Jake had sent me of the club, but I couldn't be sure.

"Hey." I poured milk over my cereal before carrying it to the small kitchen table.

Swish grabbed a dirty juice glass from the sink and sat down opposite me. He took a drag of his cigarette and blew smoke into the air. "You look a little like Jake."

"So I've been told."

"Not as friendly as he was, though."

I met Swish's dark gaze and saw humor there. "Sorry. I'm just... uncomfortable here."

Swish flicked ash into the juice glass. "I get it. A queer among bikers is kinda like... I don't know. A mouse among cats."

"How'd you know I'm queer?"

Swish shrugged. "Takes one to know one, I guess."

I smiled. "No one's chased me around trying to eat me yet."

"Even Dante?"

I raised a brow. "That would explain him calling me *babe*."

"He's bi." Swish fiddled with his cigarette as though the subject of Dante distracted him.

"Not to be rude, but you don't really seem like the rest of the club." I took a bite of cereal.

"I'm not a member. I guess you'd call me a hanger-on. But that's a story for another time." Swish took another drag of his cigarette and leaned back in his chair. I refrained from wrinkling my nose at the copious amount of smoke billowing between us, but only just. I needed to get out of there before I got lung cancer from all the second-hand smoke.

"Sucks what's going down with you and the Pistons."

That uncomfortable *my life's in danger* feeling that had begun to sink in since the night Zeke had appeared in Nikki's apartment squeezed at my stomach, and I put down my spoon.

"Oops. Sorry," Swish said. "I never was good being delicate about things. Maybe you can go back to — where was it? Rome? Until you're safe."

"Milan," I said. "I'm going to apprentice with the Manhattan Ballet. It's my dream."

"Well, that sounds pretty impressive. What does it mean, exactly?"

"Basically, it's a year shadowing the ballet company, attending every rehearsal, learning all the parts and being ready to step into any of them at a moment's notice. If I'm lucky, at the end of the year I'll be asked to join the company. After that, I'll work to be a soloist, and then a principal dancer."

Swish tucked a strand of light brown hair that had fallen from his bun behind one ear. A silver cross dangled from his earlobe, and I was pretty sure he was wearing lip gloss. His lips were unusually shaped, like gentle ripples on the water. "Guess all that dancing's where you got that rocking bod."

I laughed. "*Rocking bod?* Really? If that was a pick-up line, you definitely need a new one."

Swish smiled. "I'm not coming on to you, but I wouldn't object, if that's what you want." He winked. "Although I have a feeling we'd both be jockeying for the same position."

I laughed. "You're probably right. I'd think you have enough "rocking bods" to look at here with the Hedonists, anyway."

Swish shrugged. "A little too beefy for my taste. Except for Dante. His body is perfect."

He continued smoking, and I finished my cereal, wondering about him and Dante but not wanting to ask.

A bark from the back porch reminded me about the dogs. "When I first got here, I saw you with a different dog. How many do you have?"

"Oh, they aren't mine. I groom them. You know, wash them, clip their fur and nails, and put bows on their heads. Stuff like that."

"Really? Here?"

Swish shrugged. "Sure. Got everything set up on the back porch. I'll show you sometime. I make a decent amount of money. Keeps me from totally freeloading here. I'm squirreling away as much as I can, hoping to get my own shop. Maybe sleep in the back."

"Cool." I didn't know what Swish's story was, but I admired him for using his skills to make it in life. I got up to rinse my bowl in the sink. "You know where Zeke is? If I don't get to dance in a real studio soon, I'll go crazy."

Swish regarded me through a cloud of cigarette smoke. "Pretty sure he's in the basement working on the dryer."

I hadn't known there was a basement. I must have looked uncertain, because Swish stood.

"I'll show you."

I followed him to a door tucked beneath the stairwell, and he flipped on a light. As we descended the steps, I asked, "You called anything but Swish?"

"Not anymore." He didn't offer an explanation, and I added it to the list of things to ponder about him.

I looked around. A bare bulb hung from the ceiling, and one window high up on the wall allowed in a small amount natural light. Zeke was on his hands and knees behind the dryer. From that angle, I had a great view of his ass and found myself staring at it before jerking to attention and nudging his leg with my foot.

"I need someone to take me to the dance studio near where Nikki lives," I said.

Zeke didn't look up from what he was doing. "I'll be finished here in an hour."

"Okay. I'll get ready."

The stairs vibrated with someone descending, and Swish looked up. "Ax could probably do it."

"Ax?" I wasn't sure I wanted to know, although with this club the guy could just as well be named after his favorite body spray as his chosen implement for murder.

A man appeared from around the corner. A big man. "I can do what?"

"Morgan needs a ride somewhere."

Over six and a half feet tall, bald, with tats all over his head and arms the size of my thighs, Ax was fucking scary-looking. My thoughts must have shown on my face, for he grinned and slapped me on the back, almost knocking me into Swish. A little more good-humored force, and we both would've wound up on the floor.

"Jake's little brother. Nice to finally meet you." Ax's baritone reverberated through the room. "Where you need to go, kid?"

I opened my mouth to speak, but Zeke interrupted from behind the dryer.

"He hates bein' called a kid, and I'm taking him. Go get ready, twinkle toes."

Surprised, I glanced at Ax. "Thanks anyway." I climbed the stairs, Swish behind me.

He followed me into my room and flopped onto the bed.

"Where do you sleep?" I asked, grabbing my bag and looking through it.

"In Dante's room." At my look, he added, "just platonic. He thinks of me as a little brother." The expression on Swish's face told me he wasn't crazy about that. I guessed it would be kind of shitty to sleep a few feet from a Greek god who saw you as a sibling.

I stepped out of the sweats I'd slept in and into a pair of butter-soft jeans. I'd put on my dance garb at the studio. A motorcycle roared to life outside, a sound I was quickly getting used to.

"Hey, do you mind not smoking in here?" I asked when Swish started to light up.

He slid the cigarette back into the pack. "Sure, no problem. If you aren't a smoker, you're probably gagging here."

"Little bit."

Swish gracefully rose from the bed and crossed to the closet. "There should be a screen in here someplace." A few minutes later, he had the window open and a breeze wafting in.

21

"Thanks," I said after taking what felt like my first deep breath since I'd arrived.

"What did you do in Italy besides dance?" He flopped back onto the bed.

I sat down at the small desk.

"Nothing. I danced all the time. Well, I had other studies, but when I wasn't doing that, I was dancing."

"Bang any cute Italian guys?"

I smiled. "No. But I made out with a few."

His face crinkled. "No sex? Really?"

I rubbed at the calluses on my right foot. "I fooled around a little, but I was there to dance, not fuck. My parents paid a lot of money for me to go to the academy in Milan."

Swish ran his finger along the inseam of his jeans. "Why not here?"

I shrugged. "Milan's academy is part of the Global School of Ballet, and my parents wanted me to experience Europe." *Or out of their hair.* "Did you know my brother well?"

"No. He was busy a lot, and I spend a lot of time grooming dogs."

"What was Jake busy doing?"

Swish's eyes flicked up to mine and back down again. "Working. Dating one chick or another. He was popular with them, though he wasn't as cute as you, in my opinion. I just always wondered why he didn't live at home. Lots of the guys in the club come from bad places, but weren't your folks rich?"

"Rich doesn't always mean good. Jake and I were estranged for a long time. It was only the last couple of years we started talking."

"Yeah? How come?"

I didn't know if he was asking why we were estranged or why we'd only recently started talking. I chose the easier to answer. "Jake didn't know how to contact me until our parents died a couple years ago. My lawyer gave him my number."

Swish curled up on the bed like a cat. "I came here with Dante and wound up staying. It's not a bad place to live."

I tried to imagine living in the clubhouse. I guessed it wouldn't be awful. Better than the street.

"Who were the girls here the other night?" I'd been introduced, but all the names had gotten jumbled in my head.

"Only four are regulars. Pammy—she was the tall red-head. Angel's the small blond. Katie's Blaze's girl, and then there's Cupcake. Pink hair. She's the only one from our MC working in the business.

"Business?" I asked, thinking of the building in the lot behind the clubhouse.

Swish started to answer, but someone knocked at the door.

"Come in," I called.

Zeke stuck his head around the door. "You ready?"

"Yeah. I'll be out in a second."

He closed the door, and I turned to find Swish looking at me. "What?"

"Just wondering why Zeke's so weird around you."

"He's not weird around you?"

"He never talks to me."

"I just thought he was weird, period." I stood and picked up my bag. "I can't wait to really dance. I've tried in here, but there isn't much room. Plus, the music's probably driving you guys crazy."

Swish stood and shrugged. "I kind of like it. Brings some culture to the place. And Blaze wants you to feel comfortable here. Zeke sleeping outside your door would make anyone feel safe."

I stilled. "What do you mean, outside my door?"

"He's been sleeping on the floor in the hall since you got here," Swish said.

"Why? Where does he normally sleep?" I hadn't thought about it before.

"He was roommates with Jake. The bed's a trundle." Swish pointed beneath the bed.

I stared. "But, why is he out in the hall?"

Swish raised a brow. "You want him in here with you?"

My body went hot all over. I looked away and shrugged. "It just seems unfair, me having his room to myself while he sleeps on the floor."

"Easier to keep people out that way," Swish said. "Besides, he's probably slept in weirder places."

"You really think that rival club could get into the house?" I asked, nerves tingling.

23

"If they really wanted to, they could." Swish glanced at the open window. "I'd make sure that's closed and locked when you go to bed tonight."

I didn't want to think about it. I picked up my cell phone from where it was charging on the nightstand.

"You think it would be okay to have my friend over later?"

Swish paused, hand on the doorknob. "Sure. And try to relax. You'll be safe with Zeke."

I dialed Nikki's number.

"How would you like to see a real live motorcycle club?" I asked her when she answered.

"Really? I'm allowed to infiltrate the sacrosanct interior?"

"Evidently. Come around six and eat dinner with us."

I hung up, a small smile on my face, and went to meet Zeke.

CHAPTER THREE

Zeke

The ballet studio Morgan had directed me to was closed, but the kid had a key. Said it belonged to a friend of the family. As soon as we got in, I checked all the locks and scoped out the place before coming back to Morgan. He'd changed into a skimpy pair of skintight shorts and a tight T-shirt and had one toned leg up on the barre, stretching to music only my grandma would listen to but that I was quickly becoming accustomed to.

I studied the kid. A strand of his dark hair kept falling into his big, brown eyes. He had great bone structure, as Cupcake would say. She was always saying things like that, but with Morgan, I could see it. His face looked like it'd been chiseled from stone. His whole body was like that. Everything about the kid was long and lean: his neck, legs, fingers...

The shorts accentuated the tight swell of Morgan's ass, and my mouth dropped when he demonstrated the impressive ability to lift one leg straight in the air parallel with his body. Watching him made me inexplicably angry. Or something.

What was wrong with me? When I was around the guy, half the time I wanted to beat someone's face in and the other half I...

I couldn't finish the thought.

I'd been as bad as my old man, calling Morgan a queer and everything else at his friend's apartment. I just couldn't stop myself from saying those things when I was around him. Like I said, I was angry or... something else.

I needed a cigarette, but the prima donna had made it clear I couldn't smoke in the studio, and I wasn't about to leave him alone to go outside to light up. I played with my phone, but again and again found my eyes roaming to the strong, sleek lines of Morgan's body as he did something that made his legs look like egg beaters.

"Fuck this shit." I headed into the outer room to stare out the window.

My cell phone buzzed, and Blaze's name appeared on the screen.

"Yeah?"

"Zeke. Morgan with you?"

"Yeah, we're at some dance studio in Manhattan, and he's leaping around like a gazelle on crack."

"Be extra careful when you leave there."

"Something wrong?"

A long pause sent my blood pressure soaring. "Blaze?"

"Guess Spoons got wind of Morgan somehow. He and a few of his buddies just paid us a visit."

My heart stopped for a few beats before picking up again. "Damn. Everybody okay?"

"They broke down the front door and threw a few punches, but yeah. Ax was here, and that deterred them."

Yeah, the sight of Ax would deter anybody. Our MC usually kept a pretty low profile, but sometimes, when other MC's got on our backs, having Ax around came in handy. The guy'd been in and out of prison so many times, he pretty much ran the place when he was there. What most people didn't know was none of Ax's crimes had been for violence. The rumors he'd killed people for fun had all come from us.

I glanced over my shoulder to make sure I was still alone in the room and that the kid was still safe. I hated to think of what Spoons would do with someone like Morgan. Someone so...

My mind skidded to a halt.

"Wonder how they found out about Morgan."

"Tony worked it out. Remember we thought there was no obit? Well, the funeral home had one on their website. Short and sweet, but Morgan's name was there as the only next of kin."

"Fuck. But they didn't show up at the funeral. I'm positive about that."

"Vanessa's funeral was the same day, same time." Blaze lowered his voice. "We gotta keep him safe, Zeke. I can't let J down, but man, Spoons looked crazed. Like he hadn't slept in a week."

"Fuck."

"The kid can't go off to live at the school. He'll be a sitting duck."

"Ain't gonna be easy to convince him not to."

"He can commute, with you or someone else tailing him. Convince him, Zeke. I gotta find some leverage. I've got Tony on it, but it'll take time."

"What makes you think I can convince him? He likes you better than me."

"I take it you used your considerable charm to get him here," Blaze said wryly. "But in spite of that, he relaxes when he's around you. Seems to trust you. Talk to him. Tony will come up with something soon."

I grunted, surprised at his words. Morgan relaxed around me? Blaze was right about the course of action: the only way to avoid retribution between clubs was through blackmail. If the intel was good enough, we'd have a shot. Hopefully, Spoons had some secrets he needed to keep.

Blaze sighed into the phone. "I don't know what J was thinking, man."

"Thinking with his dick, more than likely. He wouldn't be the first. I'll see you in a while, Boss."

I disconnected, checked the lock on the door again, and went back to watching Morgan, who seemed lost in what he was doing. It was perplexing. The way he moved should have made him look girly, but there was something very masculine in the way his limbs moved.

I'd grown up thinking any man who put on slippers and leaped around a stage wasn't really a man. My father and brothers certainly would have said that. Before seeing Morgan dance, it had never occurred to me that a man could show strength as well as beauty in dance. Not that I would've been caught dead watching ballet; Pop and my brothers would have pissed themselves laughing before pulverizing me for being such a sissy.

Maybe if Ma had lived, things would have turned out different in my family, but she was long gone, and it was what it was. At least I didn't have to live in that house anymore. I owed the club for that and a lot more.

"You ready to go now?" I asked when Morgan appeared in front of me, sweat running down his neck and soaking his shirt. I hadn't even noticed the music had stopped.

Morgan didn't seem fazed by my gruffness. Maybe Blaze was right, and the kid felt relaxed around me. When I'd broken into his friend's apartment, Morgan had been scared. Hell, he would have been stupid not to have been. I hadn't really handled that situation well, but like I said — something about Morgan put me on edge. I had to admit I'd admired the way he'd fought back and tried to get away. I knew I could be intimidating — hell, I'd worked hard to be — and I hadn't toned it down much that day. But Morgan hadn't backed down.

I watched him towel off and drink half a bottle of water in one go before turning out the lights. He followed me out, not bothering to change back into street clothes except for his shoes. I was glad for that; Blaze's call had me itching to get the kid back to the protection of the clubhouse.

I scanned the dark street before leading him to the club's SUV, my hand on the small of his back.

We climbed into the car and buckled up.

"It's already 5:45," Morgan said, looking at his phone. "Hurry. I don't want Nikki to get to the clubhouse before I do."

"God, you're so bossy. And who the hell's Nicky?" I started the car and pulled away from the curb, cutting off a cab in the process. The driver blared his horn at me, and I gave him the finger.

"My friend. It was her apartment you broke into, remember? Swish said it would be okay if she came over."

I was inexplicably relieved to hear Nikki was a girl.

I turned on some rock to negate the necessity of filling the silence with small talk, constantly on the look-out for threats while I drove. Morgan sank into the seat and napped. I was glad he didn't know what had gone down while we were gone, and, in spite of Blaze asking me to talk to him, I couldn't make myself do it. I let him rest up while he could. When we reached the clubhouse, I pulled around back.

"Something wrong?" Morgan asked, turning off the radio.

"Just being cautious."

I made sure the coast was good and clear before escorting Morgan inside. He stopped in the hallway where Ax and Dante were fixing the kicked-in front door.

"What happened?"

"Got paid a visit by a rival group," Dante said. "Mind grabbing us some water from the fridge?"

Morgan looked from Dante to me before turning and walking into the kitchen.

"How bad was it?" I asked, keeping my voice low.

"Could've been worse," Ax said. "Pussies left when they saw me."

"Because you're fucking scary," Dante said. "Anyone who chops up people and puts them in pies shouldn't be messed with."

We all chuckled, knowing Ax was nothing like the stories we passed around. Ax and Dante grunted as they lifted the door into place.

"Good thing the Pistons ain't got anyone as big as you," I said to Ax.

"Aw, you say the sweetest things. You should see me in bed, sugar."

I'm sure I paled, because Dante and Ax laughed at me.

I passed Morgan with the water on my way to find Blaze.

I found him the living room with Tony and Hung. I sank into the over-sized chair and crossed my foot over my knee.

"S'up?"

"Going over possibilities," Blaze said.

Morgan appeared in the doorway just as Ax announced someone was pulling up outside. I was half out of the chair when Morgan announced it was Nikki. I'd forgotten all about her. I eased back against the cushion.

Nikki was little, pointy-chinned, and feisty. The heavy burgundy hair piled up on top of her head added another couple inches to her short stature, along with the three-inch heels on her boots. And she was still fucking tiny.

"Hi," she said, looking warily at each of us in turn. Blaze made introductions.

"Hung? Seriously?" She stared at the Latino.

"Try me, baby," Hung said.

Nikki looked amused, and I couldn't help but like her a little for it.

She gave me an interested once-over. "So, you're the one who broke into my place."

"Took advantage of the open balcony door," I corrected.

She gave me a bullshit look and turned to Blaze. I would've bet my cut the sight of him drenched her panties. Blaze tended to have that effect on women. Man, good thing Katie wasn't there to see it; she'd rip Nikki bald.

"You a dancer too?" Blaze asked Nikki.

"I was. I had a couple bad injuries and had to hang up my ballet slippers," Nikki said, and I noticed Morgan looking at her with an almost guilty expression, which I couldn't figure out. Maybe he'd dropped her or something, although I had a difficult time imagining someone as graceful as Morgan doing that.

Blaze offered Nikki a seat, and my mouth went dry when Morgan perched on the arm of my chair. I didn't understand why the kid affected me the way he did. I wasn't one to go ga-ga over people, and he was a fucking guy, for Christ's sake. It didn't make any sense. But that didn't stop my pulse from racing at him being so close.

"Tell me what's going on with Morgan," Nikki demanded.

"Morgan's brother was with a rival club member's girl when he crashed his bike," Blaze said.

"But what kind of danger is he in?"

I couldn't help but notice how Nikki talked about Morgan like she was his mom or something. Morgan didn't seem bothered by it, but it kind of pissed me off. Like maybe since I'd been given the responsibility of looking after him, she was encroaching on my territory.

"A lot," Blaze said. "We'd hoped they'd never find out about him, but thanks to an online obituary, they now know. Paid us a visit not an hour ago."

Morgan went pale, brown eyes huge. "They're the ones who broke the door?"

Blaze gave me the stink eye for not having told Morgan on the ride home. "Yeah. Came bustin' in demanding we turn you over."

"Fucking door wasn't even locked," Hung mumbled. "I'd just been outside and was coming in to get a drink. "Would it've killed them to try the knob?"

Morgan seemed to shrink. "What would they have done with me?"

Instinctively, I settled my hand on Morgan's back, and the way Morgan pressed into the touch killed me. Like he trusted me. It made me feel even more protective of him than I already did.

"Killed you, what do you think?" Hung answered, and Dante punched the Latino in the arm.

"Fucking get a censor. The kid's gonna pass out!"

I looked at Morgan, and he really did look pale as a ghost.

"I'm just... tired from dancing," he said faintly.

"This is fucking crazy," Nikki bitched. "Morgan doesn't have anything to do with that club. He barely has anything to do with this one."

"Doesn't matter," Blaze said. "Jake was fooling around with Spoons's girl. No man's gonna turn his back on that. He'll look like a fucking pussy if he does."

Nikki cleared her throat. "Could you find another term to use, please? I find that one offensive."

"Uh, sure," Blaze said, looking bewildered before sighing and turning to Morgan. "You can't go out and live on your own right now. You can stay with us. Someone will take you to the school every day."

"He can stay with me," Nikki said, wrapping an arm around Morgan's shoulders. I wanted to pry her off.

"And they'll kill him. Right after they kill you," Hung said, and I shot him a warning look.

I ran my thumb over the skin beneath where Morgan's shirt had bunched up and felt him tremble. From what was being said, or from my touch?

Nikki started to argue, but Morgan cut her off.

"He's right. I don't want to put you in danger. I guess it's okay if I stay here a while, as long as I start school as planned."

Blaze looked relieved. "It'll just be until we can find something on Spoons that we can hold over his head."

"Blackmail?" Morgan asked.

"You wanna live to toss around girls in tutus on the big stage one day?" I asked, annoyed he wasn't thinking of his safety first.

Nikki turned on me like an angry chihuahua. "The male dancers don't toss us around, you Neanderthal. It's all highly coordinated dance moves. And Morgan's well on his way to being a premiere dancer. You bikers think you're so tough. Well, I've got news for you: Morgan could crack your head like a nut using only his thighs."

The image of my head between Morgan's thighs short-circuited my brain for several beats of the clock.

Blaze coughed into his hand, and I wanted to rip the heated look right off fucking Dante's face.

"I'm sure normally Morgan is capable of taking care of himself, but you have to understand what kind of men we're talking about, here," Blaze said after a beat. "Our club's pretty benign, but I can't say the same for the Pistons."

Hung leaned forward. "These guys would think nothing of hanging pretty boy by his wrists from the ceiling, skinning him alive, and leaving him on our clubhouse porch as a message not to mess with their babes again."

Morgan's back stiffened under my hand.

"Shut up, Hung." My tone was lethal. The Latino gave me an odd look but settled back against the couch.

Blaze looked up at Morgan perched on my chair. "Don't worry; we'll protect you until we get this ironed out. And we want you to be comfortable here. Ax can even fix up the basement so you can practice your dancing. Barres, sound system, the works."

"That's not necessary. I'll get plenty of practice at the school. I'll be there most of the time, anyway." Morgan glanced down at me. "If I'm going to stay a while, Zeke needs to sleep in the room, though, and not out in the hall."

Surprised he knew about that, I said, "I'm supposed to be guarding you."

"Then do it from inside the room. God, you think just because I'm gay, I'm going to jump you? Give me a break."

"I never thought you were going to jump me," I said, voice rising. "I just wanted to give you some goddamn privacy. This has got to be tough on you as it is."

The room fell silent.

"Why don't you shower, Morgs? You're all sweaty," Nikki suggested softly.

"Will you be okay?"

"Of course."

He left the room, and I smoked a cigarette while Nikki talked to Blaze, occasionally casting disapproving glances at my cigarette.

That was just too bad; I might curb the smoking around Morgan, but this chick wasn't anyone to me.

I didn't stop to wonder what exactly Morgan was to me.

CHAPTER FOUR

Morgan

Christ, the man infuriated me. He could be such a fucking dick, and then he'd turn around and say something that totally caught me off guard. I don't even know why I'd sat so close to him in the living room, except that he made me feel safe.

Thinking about those guys from the other gang coming there to get me had my stomach hurting. I couldn't believe I was in this situation. I washed off the sweat of an hour and a half's worth of dancing, bone tired and scared. Turning off the taps, I rested my forehead against the cool tile a moment before stepping out onto the fluffy blue rug.

I shook out my wet hair, which could use a cut, and toweled off in front of the long mirror, inspecting the twin bruises on my hipbones where Zeke had slammed me to the floor of Nikki's apartment. I dropped the towel and ran my hands over them.

Remembering how it had felt to have Zeke pressed against me, I moved my fingers over my skin and through my trimmed, black pubic hair before wrapping them around my cock. Dropping my chin to my chest, I tugged and stroked, thinking about how the burly biker's erection had felt cradled between my ass cheeks.

First time he'd laid eyes on me, and he'd wanted me.

Why did that feel so good to know? His habit of staring at me, watching me so closely all the time. It did something to me.

I closed my eyes and stroked harder, imagining Zeke's grip on my erect cock instead of my own, my body tensing with impending release.

With a rush that brought a gasp from my lips, I came all over my hand and the bathroom floor, residual tremors rocking my body as I sagged against the wall. Several minutes went by before my head cleared enough for me to clean up the mess and put my clothes on, telling myself maybe now I could concentrate.

Much more relaxed than I had been before my shower, I walked down the hall, my worries of leaving Nikki alone with the bikers disappearing at the sound of her laughter punctuated by a snort. When I entered the room, she was sitting next to Blaze on the couch, her hand clamped over her mouth in embarrassment. Zeke, Hung, and Dante were gone.

"Happens every time," I said. "Sometimes she even does it in her sleep."

I danced back to avoid the pointy toe of Nikki's boot and glanced around.

"Zeke went to Home Depot to get something Ax needs for the door," Blaze told me.

I cleared my throat, embarrassed I'd been caught looking for him, and sat down on the couch next to Nikki.

"You sure you want me to stay here? It's going to be a real pain in the ass for somebody to go with me to rehearsals every day."

"J was the best friend I had in the world," Blaze said. "There's nothing I wouldn't do for him, and therefore for you."

I worked my bottom lip between my teeth, sadness settling over me. "I still can't believe he's gone. I guess after talking long distance for so long, I still expect him to be here waiting for me."

"I wish he were," Blaze said, looking away, and an almost tangible grief rose in the room, filling the air until Swish walked out of the kitchen wearing an apron that read Kiss the Cook.

He looked from one sad face to another. "Uh, dinner's ready."

We stood and shuffled into the dining room, where Hung and Dante were already seated.

"Smells great, what is it?" Blaze asked.

"Tuna casserole," Swish said, uncovering the dish.

"One of my favorites," Nikki said politely as she took a seat beside me.

"Hope you washed the mutts off your hands before you cooked," Hung said, "though I'm so hungry, I'd probably eat it anyway."

"I saw that standard poodle," Dante told Swish, as though to soften Hung's words. "You did a great job on him."

"On her, and thanks." Swish smiled at Dante, and for a moment they seemed unaware of the rest of us until Hung moaned with appreciation over his bite of casserole. I had to admit, it was pretty tasty, and I wasn't a big fan of tuna.

Hung ruffled Swish's hair, pulling much of it free from its elastic band. "You did good."

Swish pushed him away and moved from the table to fix his hair. "Like I want or need your approval, you ingrate."

Hung laughed and took another large bite of casserole.

"Where is everyone?" I asked after a few moments of refilling plates and passing salt and napkins.

"Work, dates. Ax went to a nearby bar," Dante answered. "Some of the girls went to party."

Hung dug his elbow into Blaze's ribs. "Sex toys. Katie'll come back with a bag of 'em."

Blaze didn't look particularly excited at the prospect.

Dante asked Nikki a few polite questions, and she told them a little about the bookstore and her boyfriend, Paul.

I enjoyed the relative quiet and the fact I didn't have to say much. The good feeling I'd gotten from my shower and quick jack off session was wearing off, and my stomach rebelled, but I managed to eat.

After dinner, Nikki and I went to my room, cuddled up on the bed, and watched a Netflix movie on my computer.

It was late when she rolled to her feet and announced, "I'm heading home. I'm beat."

I yawned and followed her through the house.

Blaze was stretched out on the couch watching TV. He waved goodbye to Nikki.

"Nice girl," he said when I returned to the living room after seeing her out.

"Yeah. The nicest. We've been friends a long time."

Blaze turned off the television. "Morgan, I want to talk to you about J."

I sat down beside Blaze and met his steady gaze, the drowsiness that had set in during the movie clearing away.

"Did he ever tell you why he left home?" Blaze asked me.

"No, but I remember he and Dad always fought, and I think a part of the reason our parents sent me to Milan was to get me away from Jake's influence. At least, I used to think that. Lately, I've been wondering if they just wanted to get rid of me."

"I hope you know J would have never done anything that would have gotten you hurt."

"How long did you know my brother?" I asked.

"We became friends our freshman year of high school."

I frowned. That was much longer than I'd thought. "Jake was a junior when he left home. Why didn't I ever meet you?"

Blaze rubbed the back of his neck. "I was from the wrong side of the tracks. No way would your parents have been happy I was Jake's friend."

I immediately realized the truth in that and was ashamed at what snobs my parents had been.

"When my older brother died, and I took over the club," Blaze continued, "J began spending more and more time here. Before that, he'd known I belonged to a motorcycle club, but not the specifics. I taught him to ride a Harley, and he became a prospect, living a double life—half here at the club, and half at his fancy house with his country club friends. When Jake got the club tat, the shit hit the fan. Your old man said it was either the MC or home, and Jake chose the club."

I let that sink in. I always thought the MC had taken Jake in off the streets after our father had kicked him out. That he'd had no choice. When the truth was Jake had chosen to leave home. He'd chosen the club over us.

I felt sick.

Blaze patted my leg. "Jake loved you. Man, all he did was worry about you, but he couldn't stand living with your folks anymore. After he left, your parents would have gone nuts if he'd tried to talk to you. But he went to all your performances at the school while you were still here."

Surprised, I raised my eyes to meet Blaze's. "He did?"

"Yeah. I went to a few of them too. It killed J when your folks sent you away."

I swallowed hard, gut twisting with a long-buried question. "Did he... think I was weird for dancing ballet?"

Blaze scoffed. "Hell, no! He was so proud of you. For your dancing and for not selling your shares in the company. He said you had bigger balls than he did."

That brought a wistful smile to my face.

"I'd always wished he was around," I whispered.

"Leaving you was J's only regret. He thought about going back home, sucking it up to your dad, more than once, but he couldn't let go of the club. We'd all become too close, and he was his own person, far from the one your folks wanted him to be."

"I thought Jake just didn't care enough to make the effort to keep in touch with me," I admitted. "I mean, he explained that wasn't the case when he called me in Milan. But that's what I'd thought for a long time." I realized I'd needed this — reassurance from Jake's best friend that what my brother had told me had been the truth. That Jake had really cared about me.

Blaze wrapped his arm around my neck, much like I imagined Jake might have done if he were there. "J didn't want to mess up your dream. After your folks died, he changed his mind, though. Said he didn't want you to feel all alone in the world. He contacted that lawyer friend and begged for your number."

Tears clogged my throat, and I swallowed hard several times.

Blaze stood. "I'll leave you alone, but if there's anything you want to talk about, I'm here. Okay? I just thought you should know all that stuff."

I sat in the living room a long time, just staring into space, feeling numb. The girls returned, Katie with a large pink bag in her hand with the words Allora's Secrets written on it in black script.

"Blaze is in his room," Hung told her, casting Dante a knowing leer.

Sometime later, I heard Zeke come in from the garage and wash his hands. A moment later, his boots planted themselves in my line of vision.

"What's the matter? You look like someone stole your favorite tutu," he said.

The melancholy and self-pity I'd been stewing in morphed into anger, and I stood and pushed past him. "Would you just stop with the smart-ass comments?" I snapped before heading to my room.

I flopped onto the bed that had been my brother's and proceeded to cry for the first time since I'd found out he'd been killed.

CB♥SO

Hours later, after I'd pulled myself up and brushed my teeth, I saw Dante headed for his bedroom with a girl whose total outfit wasn't any bigger than two dinner napkins. A minute later, and Swish showed up in my doorway.

"You okay?"

I nodded.

"Mind if I take the trundle tonight? Dante's probably going to be at it till morning."

Sounds of the bed knocking against the other side of the wall punctuated the statement. Dante sure didn't waste any time. Swish seemed to be deliberately ignoring the noise.

"Sorry," I said. "I told Zeke to take the trundle. I didn't like the idea of him sleeping on the floor in the hall."

Swish shrugged. "I can sleep on the couch, or maybe on Blaze's floor, if Katie leaves."

"They pretty serious?" I asked.

"Katie'd like to think so."

"But?"

Swish shrugged. "Blaze never gets serious about anybody. In another couple months, she'll be gone, and there'll be another chick in her place. That's the way it's always been. He never hits the year mark with any of them."

Swish leaned against the bedroom door. "So, you're gonna bunk down with ole Zeke, huh?"

I narrowed my eyes at him. "He'll be sleeping on the trundle."

"I've seen the way he looks at you."

"He doesn't look at me any certain way."

"He looks at you like he wants to climb into your tights with you."

At the mention of tights, my back stiffened. "I'm sick of people making fun of me."

"I'm not making fun. I think it's cool you're a dancer. Not to mention hot."

"Yeah, well, a lot of people would disagree with you. But dancing's fucking hard work, and anyone who doesn't believe that should try it sometime."

Swish put up his hands in surrender. "Hey, no need to tell me. I respect you for it. And Zeke seems to appreciate the way you move."

Swish smiled knowingly. "Wouldn't be the first time a straight man changed teams."

I shook my head, unwilling to let Swish jerk me down that road. I was attracted to Zeke, but I knew it was a lost cause and wasn't willing to let myself entertain the idea he might be into me. That way led to rejection, and I'd had enough of that in my life. I shucked off my jeans and Swish and I exchanged goodnights before he shut the door, and I crawled into bed.

Maybe Zeke wouldn't even sleep on the trundle. Maybe he'd rather sleep on the floor in the hall than next to a gay ballet dancer. The thought hurt.

Sometime later, the sound of the hidden bed being pulled out woke me. I pretended to stay asleep, cracking my eyes open just enough to watch from under my lashes as Zeke peeled off his T-shirt and stripped out of his jeans. His body was incredible, big and brawny, broad shoulders tapering down to a narrow waist. Fuck, he was gorgeous.

Zeke pulled back the covers on the low bed and lay down. I hadn't closed the curtains, and moonlight shone through the window onto his ripped physique, the curve of his cock clearly outlined through the thin material of his white briefs. God, and he was semi-hard. Was that normal for him, or did it have something to do with me? I wanted to know for certain.

Wide awake now and unbearably curious, I slowly rolled toward the window onto my stomach, bringing up my leg in a motion that pulled off the sheet from the rest of me. Now my ass was in full view, only a pair of red bikini briefs between it and the open air. I heard Zeke's head turn against the pillow, felt his gaze on me.

I waited, breathing deeply and regularly as though in sleep, which wasn't easy with my heart beating as hard as it was. I heard movement, as though Zeke shifted on the bed. A couple agonizing moments later, the telltale slapping and ragged breathing of a man jerking one off filled the room.

The thought of Zeke masturbating to the sight of my ass had my cock leaking. I listened, heard Zeke's breath hitch, and had to carefully move my hand so I could squeeze the base of my dick to keep from coming.

A few minutes later, I heard Zeke get up and clean off. I waited a long time in silence before sliding my hand into my briefs and stroking myself, moving my palm over the head of my cock while biting my bottom lip. When Zeke began to snore, I quickened my pace, strangling the cry that tried to rip from my throat when I came.

Flopping onto my back, I looked up at the dark ceiling. I had my answer: Zeke wanted me. But what the fuck did it prove? It only made me want him more, but going after him would be a mistake. Straight, gay, or bi-curious, the guy had issues with his sexuality. Even if he did sleep with me, he'd regret it right after. Every gay guy learned early to stay far away from a closeted man, no matter how much we'd like to believe we could be the one to bring him out. And didn't I have enough problems without adding to them?

I turned my head on the pillow and looked down at Zeke. The moonlight fell on the little devil face tattooed on his upper arm—the same that was featured in the middle of the back of the club's leather vests, or cuts. The sight of it reminded me that more than Zeke's sexuality lay between us. We were from different worlds. Just because he made me feel safe and secure didn't mean anything. I'd been without anyone for most of my maturing years; it was no wonder I yearned for such feelings.

Eventually, I drifted off to sleep and dreamed of motorcycles and muscles. When I awoke in a sweat, my morning wood fighting to get out of my briefs, the trundle had been put away, and I was alone.

CHAPTER FIVE
Zeke

I couldn't deny my attraction to Morgan Wentworth anymore — not after bringing myself off to the sight of his ass in a pair of tight red briefs. Holy shit, I'd wanted to cram myself inside him so bad. And that fucking terrified me. Since when did I fantasize about having my dick in a man's ass? I'd come in an embarrassing amount of time just looking at him. Thank God he was a deep sleeper.

Hearing him crying in the bedroom had torn me up. I'd told myself the kid was grieving, and my "tutu" comment had just been a catalyst, but I'd still felt like shit. I'd purposely waited until the light had been off a while before creeping into the room and undressing for bed. Lying on the trundle, I'd smelled Morgan's alluring scent in the air. Did the little fuck wear cologne to bed, or did he naturally smell like a spice closet? I wanted to know what he smelled like everywhere, and what the fuck did that mean?

What I needed was pussy, wet and tight. It had been too long, and I was obviously in withdrawal; that had to be the explanation for my bizarre reaction to Morgan.

It was Saturday, and the scent of cooking meat drifted in through the back door from where Dante stood flipping burgers on the grill. Nikki was there, and she was drinking like there was no tomorrow. Chick her size, I couldn't believe she wasn't sliding under the table by now. Morgan, wearing a ripped pair of jeans and a navy sweatshirt that shouldn't make me hard but did, sat in the dining room talking to her and offering tissues.

"What happened there?" I asked Swish, who'd left the two to come and sit in front of the TV with me.

"Nikki broke up with her boyfriend," Swish said.

"If she did the breaking up, why's she bawling like that?" Hung asked from where he was sizing up a pool shot while Tony waited.

"Break-ups are hard," Swish said. "But neither of you would know that, since you don't exactly date. Not to mention, you probably consider a text message a good way to break it off with someone."

"I take offense to that remark," Hung said. "I've been known to go on more than one date with the same person."

Swish made a face. "I'll bet neither of you have ever experienced a real relationship."

He had me there, so I wasn't going to argue, although Hung continued to.

My experience with women before the club was next to nil, but after, when I'd bulked up and convinced myself I was a tough biker, screwing girls became my way of proving that to myself.

I'd never been a part of the business; Blaze wouldn't allow it. He'd said I could do more than get naked for a camera, although he used to do it before the site really took off. All I had was what my pop had taught me—tinkering with cars. Luckily, I was good at it and quickly became well-known in the area. Fixing cars and being part of the club had given me something to be proud of. Starting a relationship hadn't even entered my mind.

Cupcake walked through the front door, a few girls trailing behind her. Spoons hadn't been around since the day he'd come looking for Morgan, but all of us knew it was only a matter of time. I'd talked about it with Dante, and we both thought the Pistons most likely would try to snatch up the kid between the clubhouse and the relative safety of his dance school. Still, we had a couple guys posted outside just in case.

Long-nailed fingers ran down my arm before curling around my hand. "Hey, how've you been, stranger?"

I winked at the little bleached blond everyone called Jojo before taking a swig of beer. I'd hooked up with her a few times in the past, but it had been a good while. Maybe she was just what I needed.

"Better now that you're here."

Jojo smiled and tugged at my hand, drawing me closer. Her perfume stung my nose. I'd never realized it was cheap until that moment.

"I've missed you, Zeke."

I sincerely doubted that, but I went along with it, reminding myself I'd gone too long without my chief affirmation. No wonder I was having weird thoughts about Morgan.

The top of her head barely came to my collarbone. I petted the curve of her back with my free hand, and she pressed her small, perky breasts against my chest. She wasn't wearing a bra.

"Why don't we have a chat in my room?" I said, wrapping my arm around her shoulders and guiding her down the hall. She smiled and nodded. Before I'd finished closing and locking the door, Jojo was on her knees and had my cock out. A cool breeze blew through the screen in the open window. I could hear Skitz and Bullseye out on the porch laughing about something.

My heartbeat picked up as she propped my nuts on the waistband of my boxer briefs and licked the tip of my cock with her studded tongue.

"That's it," I said, succumbing to the feeling of a warm mouth around my dick. Jojo sure knew what she was doing, but my cock was responding more to the unbidden image in my mind of Morgan on his knees, taking me in. I didn't have it in me to try to expel it. I was on the fast road to release, with an ETA of less than three minutes. Picturing Morgan's big brown eyes staring up at me while he gagged on my rod, I came with a hoarse cry.

Fuck, that felt *so mother-fucking good*. As the last pulse shot down Jojo's throat, I opened my eyes and smiled, not even embarrassed at how fast I'd come.

"Thanks, babe. I needed that."

"My pleasure," she said, getting to her feet while I tucked myself back in.

Feeling like I ought to return the favor, I tried to decide the fastest way to do it, but Cupcake saved me the trouble by calling for Jojo from the hallway.

"See ya later," Jojo said to me with a wink and opened the bedroom door. I headed for the backyard, the smell of burgers drawing me over to where Dante stood filling plates by the barbecue.

I grinned at him as he placed a thick burger on my bun. "I'm starved."

"There's more where that came from." Dante took a swig of beer with his free hand.

I found a place to sit in the shade and looked around as I ate. Ax sat on a lounge chair, Cupcake next to him. Foghorn was telling a group of people an animated story accompanied by a lot of rowdy laughter. I looked around for Blaze and spotted him on the back patio having what looked like a hell of an argument with Katie. I put a few potato chips on my burger and took a bite.

"Mind if we sit here?"

Nikki stood by my chair, Morgan a few steps behind her. He didn't look at me.

"Free country." I continued eating. Already, my cock was responding to Morgan being near. I positioned my plate over the bulge.

Nikki had fixed her make-up but seemed subdued. She sat in one of the low beach chairs near mine, and Morgan gracefully sank into the seat farthest from me. The chance for my dick to calm down should have made me happy, but it didn't. I liked it when Morgan wanted to be near me.

"Work up an appetite?" Morgan asked, big brown eyes suddenly staring me down.

I licked mustard off my bottom lip, and damn if Morgan didn't shift his gaze to my mouth. Just the thought of what he might be thinking had me hot and bothered. I took a long drink of beer from the cold bottle I'd snatched from the cooler.

"Yeah, I guess," I said, not sure what Morgan meant by the question.

"I have my first class on Monday."

I nodded. I knew that; the day before, we'd spent hours at the academy squaring things away.

"I asked Hung to take me."

I met Morgan's gaze unwaveringly. "I'm taking you."

Morgan looked away.

Nikki glanced from one of us to the other before giving up and starting on the pile of macaroni salad on her plate.

"Hung said he'd take me," Morgan said.

"Well, he ain't. I am." I was pissed. We'd squared it away the day before; I'd be with him Monday. "You know I planned to do it, so why'd you ask him?"

Morgan shrugged and studied his salad. I went back to my burger. I wasn't going to argue about this; I was taking him, and that was that.

A few minutes went by with the three of us chewing in silence while all around, people laughed and chatted. A couple people started throwing a Frisbee.

"What's stuck up your ass?" I asked, unable to take it anymore.

Morgan looked at me, and my face went hot, because of course I started thinking of putting my dick up his ass.

Fucking faggot. My dad's voice in my head startled me. He used to say that all the time about any guy who didn't seem completely masculine in his eyes.

Morgan's mouth whitened around the edges, and he tossed his plate onto the grass before rising in one fluid movement and striding toward the house on long legs I desperately wanted to feel locked around my hips. *What was wrong with me?*

I took another long drink of my beer, trying to wash down my last bite of burger.

"Why do you have to be such a shit to him?"

I cut my eyes to Nikki. I'd forgotten she was even there.

Embarrassed, I reacted nastily. "How come you didn't follow Ballerina Barbie inside?"

She pointed her plastic fork at me. "That right there. Why do you call him those names? Morgan's worked long and hard to get where he is. Being asked to apprentice for the Manhattan Ballet is a huge deal. And now he has all this gang shit hanging over him, and he can't even enjoy the honor."

"We're not a gang," I muttered, picking off chunks of bun and tossing them to a nearby squirrel. Who the hell bought buns with sesame seeds? Fucking Swish, probably. "We're a club."

"Potato, po-tah-to." Nikki stabbed at the macaroni on her plate. "You think he's had it easy."

I sighed. "Okay, I get it. Ballet is hard."

"Not just that." Her amber eyes met mine. "You think because he has money, everything is great for him, but that isn't true. Morgan's parents were controlling shit heads who sent him to Europe when he was just a kid. Alone. Then they died. He's lost his brother—someone he'd looked forward to finally getting to know

46

better — and he's scared for his life. So, maybe you can cut him some slack."

I looked at her and gave a curt nod. Maybe I could.

Deciding we'd concentrated on me enough, I turned the tables. "How come you broke up with your boyfriend?"

Nikki's eyes shuttered. "None of your fucking business."

I shrugged. "Just wondered. The way you were crying your eyes out, you'd think he dumped you."

Nikki looked toward the house at nothing in particular, as far as I could tell. Or maybe she was super interested in the aluminum siding.

She was silent so long, I resumed eating, wondering if Morgan would come back out.

"Paul's too good for me," Nikki finally said.

"Huh?" The second half of my burger fell into mushy pieces on my plate. I sucked mustard off my thumb.

"He's a great guy. Too great. I'm not good enough for him."

"You dumped him because he's too good for you?" I shook my head. Chicks were so weird.

"I'd only hurt him in the end," she said.

"How long have you been together?" I asked.

"A little over a year."

"Man, that's cold."

Nikki gathered up the trash. "I'm trying to do the right thing."

"Whatever. You can tell yourself that, but in the end, you dumped a guy you've been with a long time."

Nikki's eyes met mine. "You're a real bastard, you know that?" She walked away, and I waited for her to get out of earshot before I muttered my agreement.

CHAPTER SIX

Morgan

I lay in bed, Zeke snoring softly on the trundle next to me. We hadn't spoken since the backyard. The brief image I'd gotten of a girl on her knees in front of Zeke kept replaying in front of my closed eyelids. I'd gone out on the porch to give Skitz and Bullseye a couple of cold beers and a noise through the open bedroom window had prompted me to peek in. I really wished I hadn't.

The jealousy burning inside me wouldn't let up. I wanted to hit something. Nikki hadn't known why I was so put out when I returned, and I wasn't going to tell her; she'd only say aloud what I wasn't yet ready to admit. And then Zeke had started up with the names again. We'd spent the entire day before together, and he hadn't called me Twinkle Toes or Tinkerbell once. We'd had a good time. He'd told me about what a light-weight he'd been as a kid and how he hadn't beefed up until he was in his teens and had left home. The story had ended there, but I'd felt like we'd gotten a little closer.

Despite what I'd told myself about Zeke, I'd managed to develop a crush on him. Seeing him with that girl had been like a slap in the face, harshly reminding me that he was straight. I was a fool.

After Nikki had left the barbecue, Hung had sought me out and told me Zeke was going to be the one to go with me tomorrow, and that was that. I wasn't dumb enough to think Zeke wanted to take me; Blaze had probably given Zeke the duty, and Zeke didn't want to hand it off to someone else; but I wasn't looking forward to riding in the car with him or seeing him all day long. I sighed and rolled onto my side to face the window. Away from Zeke. I didn't want to look at him, all spread out on the bed with his shirt hiked up and eight-pack rippling in the moonlight. Fuck that. I was done torturing myself.

Rhythmic pounding started up against the wall of Dante's room. I wondered if Swish was sleeping on the couch or if Blaze hadn't come home, and Swish had taken his room.

In spite of the noise and everything going on in my head, I finally started drifting off when a sound behind me brought my eyes open again. I froze, listening. Zeke rustled around, breathing erratically. I looked over my shoulder at the trundle. He jerked in his sleep, a frown on his face, and muttered something.

I rolled over and touched his shoulder. To my horror, his face crumpled and a sob escaped his lips. I was so surprised, I just hung there, half off the bed, arm suspended over his head. When Zeke began to shake, I bit my lip, wondering what kind of dream he was having. What made a tough guy whimper in his sleep? He'd probably be embarrassed as hell to know I was witnessing it. I thought about rolling over again, but the next sob brought me down on the bed with him.

"Shh," I crooned, stroking Zeke's soft blond hair. "It's okay." I was a little afraid of the reaction I'd get if Zeke woke up, but I wasn't willing to let him suffer through a nightmare by himself.

But Zeke didn't wake up. He stopped trembling and snuggled against me like he belonged there, body warm and solid. I kept stroking his hair until he sank into a deeper and dreamless sleep.

I lay staring at the moon's progress across the ceiling, pretending the last five minutes hadn't completely undone the sermon I'd just finished giving myself. Every breath I took brought the scent of Zeke's sleep-warm sweat into my nostrils. I'd crossed into unknown territory. All my make-out sessions with boys had been just that — kisses and fumbled touches in back rooms at the academy, always truncated by dance commitments. I hadn't dated, had certainly never laid down on a bed with someone and held them, their hair tickling my chin and the weight of their body firm against mine. The whole experience was so emotionally satisfying, I wanted it to go on forever.

And I was hard. Of course I was. Zeke's body was amazing and so much of it was touching mine, my cock couldn't help but notice. Still, more than his muscles beneath my fingers and the sight of his ass covered only by a pair of navy boxer briefs, it was Zeke's cheek against my chest, his breath falling on my skin, his arm draped around my waist, and his leg pressed against mine that undid me.

Intimacy. Something I'd never had with anyone, not even Nikki. Certainly not with my parents. I ran my hand over Zeke's back, the cotton of his shirt soft beneath my fingers, and pressed a kiss to his head. He didn't wake up, and I didn't want him to. A yawning emptiness welled inside me, and I gently eased out from under the sleeping man and returned to my own bed, because I couldn't torture myself like that. It was easier not to miss something you never had in the first place. Except I had had it. Tasted what it was like. A bottomless cavern of loneliness opened up inside me, and sleep didn't come again for a very long time.

⋘⋙

The following week was hectic. I'd gotten permission from the academy to have a bodyguard with me, and, not wanting to alarm anyone, the administration had insisted Zeke pose as a reporter doing a story on the Manhattan Ballet. While a good cover, this necessitated it always be Zeke who accompanied me, and he was sure to grow tired of the tedious twelve-hour days. His constant presence also meant I probably wasn't going to get rid of my infatuation with the biker anytime soon.

The company was in the middle of rehearsals for Swan Lake, and while I was engrossed in trying to memorize every part from Prince Siegfried down to the cygnets, Zeke watched me and our surroundings like he expected a hoard of bikers to appear out of nowhere and gun me down. My fear over the visit from the Steel Pistons had faded with time, and Zeke's vigilance seemed a little over the top.

"Cool it a little, would you?" I asked him during a break.

"What are you talking about?" Zeke asked.

"You're supposed to be a reporter—you should be watching me, not scanning the room and exits."

Zeke leaned in close, and my nerves lit up. "I'm keeping you safe. I don't care what they told people."

"God, that reporter's hot," Jon, one of the three other male apprentices, whispered when rehearsal resumed. We sat on the floor of the Creative Arts Center studio, and Jon passed me my water bottle.

I glanced over at Zeke where he stood a few feet away. In spite of his words, he did seem to be trying to fit in a little more. He'd taken out a pad and paper and scribbled on it every so often. He'd been dressing for the part of reporter, and I had to admit he looked amazing in a button-down shirt and dark jeans. I'd seen more than one dancer cast admiring looks his way since we'd arrived a week ago.

I shrugged. "I guess."

"You guess?" Jon shook his head. Tall and slender with auburn hair and hazel-green eyes, Jon was boyishly cute as well as a genuinely nice guy. He'd immediately taken on the task of helping me settle in, and I appreciated that more than I could say. I was nervous, especially with Elias Brainard, the Master in Chief, always watching us. I'm not sure what Brainard was looking for exactly, as most of what we did was watch the company dance, but when he showed up, I could always feel his eyes on me.

During rehearsals, I remained focused, aware an apprentice could be called to dance any part at a moment's notice and not knowing the steps would spell disaster. Not everyone would be offered a contract after their year was up, and I was determined to be one who would. During breaks, I practiced steps with the others. Class time meant more dancing, so by the time we left the Center at night, we apprentices were as wiped out as the company dancers.

"What's not to like about blond and built? He must do some serious working out."

I shrugged. "He's okay."

"He sure spends a lot of time watching you."

I'd prepared for this. "He's focusing his article on the experience of one new apprentice. Since I'm just now entering the program, I was the perfect choice."

"Lucky you," Jon said.

To the relief of my growling stomach, the ballet master called a halt to rehearsal for lunch. Zeke began chatting with one of the female core dancers, although he continued to watch me.

Jon unwrapped a sandwich and passed me half. I did the same. He'd brought ham and turkey, and I'd managed to find some peanut butter and honey in the clubhouse kitchen.

"Too bad you'll be doing this until next September. I wish I could get my nine in before next June, but as a male dancer, that's unlikely," Jon said.

Apprentices were required to dance in some capacity in eight productions a season, which could mean numerous parts; if we danced a ninth, we'd automatically be brought into the company. Otherwise, it would be a full year no matter when we began and then the decision would be made whether we were in or out. Lesser male roles make dancing a ninth production more unlikely for males than for females, as we replaced performers who were sick or injured. My late entrance pretty much guaranteed I'd be doing the whole year.

"Maybe they'll scrap it and decide to do an all-male Swan Lake like they did in London," I joked.

Jon smiled. "We should be so lucky."

Lunch ended way too soon. Our hours were brutal, ten to ten and sometimes longer, six days a week. For Zeke's sake, I hoped things with the Pistons got settled quickly, although sometimes I thought I'd miss him. When he managed to relax, he could be entertaining company.

By the time things wrapped up that night, I was dragging. I slipped on street shoes and threw on in a sweater, as the evenings were becoming chilly. Zeke waited for me by the door looking as fresh as he had that morning. I didn't know how he did it.

The moon hung large and round in the sky, outshining the street lamps, and there was a slight nip in the air. We'd waited until most everyone had dispersed, as we were riding together and that might seem odd considering Zeke's cover as a reporter. Zeke stuck close to me as we walked to the SUV – a good thing since I was weaving a bit from fatigue.

"Ready to quit yet?" I asked him through a yawn after I'd buckled into the passenger seat. "This has got to be boring as hell for you."

"Hear me complaining?"

My head hurt, and I was irritable. I'd really hoped all this would have been cleared up by now. "You're not even paid to do this. What makes you so willing to spend all day every day staring at me? What do you even get out of it?"

"Would you quit worrying about me?"

I sighed. "I just want to understand."

"We do things in the club we don't wanna do. It's part of it."

"What do you mean? Part of what?"

Zeke drove away from the Arts Center toward East 65th Street.

"Part of a family. For most of us, the club's all we got. I'm doing this for Jake, because he's not here to do it himself, and for Blaze, who feels responsible for you but can't keep an eye on you himself."

"If Jake were here, none of this would be necessary."

Zeke looked at me. "And you're pretty ticked about that, aren't you?"

I really was. Bitterness had been stewing in me ever since I'd found out about it. "Can you blame me? Why did Jake have to go and do something so stupid? Get himself killed, and with a rival MC's girlfriend on the back of his bike?"

"I'm guessing he was in love," Zeke said.

"Always something," I mumbled.

"What?" Zeke glanced at me, brow raised, before turning his attention back to the road.

If I wasn't so tired, I wouldn't let my emotions get the best of me, but as it was, I blurted, "He's no different than our parents. There was always something or someone to put ahead of me." As soon as the words were out, I felt like a sulking child, and I expected Zeke to make fun of me for it. Instead, he surprised me.

"I don't think he realized what he was getting into. I definitely don't think he'd thought of the possible repercussions on you, or else he never would have taken the chance. Jake and I weren't close, but we shared a room. I know how much he was looking forward to seeing you, kid."

I stared out the window, trying to get my emotions in check. Zeke's words helped to soothe the pain I'd been feeling, thinking Jake might not have cared as much as he'd led me to believe in our long-distance phone chats. When I felt calmer, I changed the subject.

"Where's your real family?"

"The club's my real family." Just like that, Zeke shut me down. Evidently, it was okay to lay me bare, but not so much him.

Exhaustion getting the best of me, I leaned back and closed my eyes, drifting.

The first shots sounded like fireworks. When Zeke yelled for me to get onto the floorboard, I snapped out of my doze and undid my seatbelt with shaking hands. Mind muddled, I crouched between the seat and the dash.

"What's going on?"

"They're shooting at us, that's what. Hold on and stay the fuck down!"

"Who's shooting at us?"

"The fucking Pistons, who else?"

While Zeke wove in and out of traffic, I cringed at every gunshot, unwilling to believe this was really happening and expecting the SUV to careen off the road any second. Someone was shooting. At me. Because they wanted me dead. It was terrifying and unreal and there was absolutely nothing I could do about it.

Zeke tossed his cell phone at me. "Call Blaze. He's number one on speed dial. Tell him what's going down."

Hands trembling, I did as Zeke ordered. When Blaze answered, I could barely get a word out.

"Zeke?"

"No, uh..."

"Morgan? Is that you?"

I tried again. "Yeah."

"Put Zeke on."

"He's driving. They're sh-shooting at us."

"Where are you?"

I looked at Zeke. His face was tense as he concentrated on staying on the road while a car to the left got perilously close.

"Where are we?"

"FDR Drive toward Brooklyn," Zeke said.

I repeated the words to Blaze.

"Dante's not too far from there. Would've escorted you home if something hadn't come up. Probably a fucking ruse to get him out of the way. Dammit! I should've seen this coming."

"Dante's close," I told Zeke.

"Stay down and out of sight, Morgan," Blaze said.

"I am." I clutched the phone with a sweaty hand. My head bumped against the dash of the SUV as another volley of shots rang out, and Zeke wove in and out of traffic. Didn't these people care about innocent bystanders? The back side window shattered and the vehicle filled with the sound of rushing air, honking horns, and screeching tires.

"Morgan, fucking stay down!" Zeke yelled.

I ducked back as far as I could, but there wasn't a lot of room. "What if they shoot you in the head?" I yelled back, sick at the thought of barreling full-speed into a guardrail as Zeke's brains splattered onto my body. Bile rose in my throat, and I clapped a hand over my mouth.

"Then we're fucking dead," Zeke said. "But it ain't me they're aiming for, so stay fucking down!"

I heard a motorcycle engine before several more shots split the air.

"Dante's after 'em." Zeke slowed down, and the Harley roared past. In the distance, the sound of sirens started up.

Another minute passed. "Can I get up now?" I asked.

"Yeah."

We were crossing the Brooklyn Bridge.

I looked behind us. "What about Dante?"

"He'll be okay. He knows what he's doing."

I turned in my seat and stared blankly out the windshield while Zeke kept glancing from the road to the rearview mirror. In less than fifteen minutes, we were pulling up to the clubhouse. Blaze came off the front porch at a run, several of the guys spilling out the door behind him. Before I knew it, I was hauled from the car and examined.

"I'm okay," I said. The sudden weight of Zeke's hand on the back of my neck made me realize I was repeating the words over and over again, and I clamped my mouth shut.

Blaze wrapped his arm around my shoulders. "Let's get you inside."

The group surrounded me, and we walked up the porch steps and inside the clubhouse.

"Fuck, that was close." Zeke flopped onto the couch and began relating what had happened. I dropped down beside him.

Hung wrapped a blanket around my shoulders.

"You okay, kid?" he asked.

I nodded, trying hard to control my shaking. I was so out of my element, it wasn't even funny. My teeth clacked together like castanets. I looked at the large front window, wondering if bullets would shatter the glass any minute. We could all be dead in a matter of seconds. What kind of nightmare was I living?

As Zeke calmly detailed what had happened to Blaze and the others, Swish brought me a cup of water, and I drank it before sinking back into the cushions. Without thinking, I curled up and laid my head in Zeke's lap. I was exhausted, and tremors still ran through me. My body was shutting down, turning off. It needed recharging, but my mind was still going a million miles a minute. Had I really just been shot at? Multiple times? These people would go to such great lengths to kill someone they'd never even met?

Jake, why did you get mixed up with one of them?

Not too long after, Dante blew into the clubhouse, high on adrenaline and animated as fuck, and the whole conversation started up again. I didn't take in any of it but was comforted by the steady cadence of the voices around me. Surprised Zeke hadn't pushed my head off his lap yet, I began to relax, calmed by the familiar scent of the biker.

"He's out," I heard Dante say.

"Probably in shock." Blaze.

"You want me to carry him into the bedroom?" Hung asked.

"Naw," Zeke said, and I was just cognizant enough to wonder at it. "Let the kid rest. I'll just chill here for a while."

The sound of shuffling feet exiting the room was followed by doors closing. The TV clicked on. I did sleep then, surfacing now and then to a game show, then a drama, then an infomercial. At one point I was aware of Zeke stroking my hair and thought I must be dreaming. Another time, I was sure I heard him speak.

"Don't worry, kid. I'm not gonna let anything happen to you."

"Not a kid," I mumbled back and heard Zeke chuckle, low and much too sexy.

I awoke the following morning, still on the couch with the blanket spread over me, alone, as though it had all been nothing more than a dream.

CHAPTER SEVEN
Zeke

A smarter guy would take a step back. Let one of the other members watch the kid, at least for a couple days until I could get my head on straight. The Pistons weren't likely to strike again so soon. Dante had fucked up more than one of their bikes in the chase. But as my father had been fond of telling me, I wasn't smart.

The events of the other night haunted me, replacing my usual nightmares of my brother Steve's death. In this dream, I held Morgan's body riddled with bullets, howling out a grief deeper than I thought I could possess, while dark, empty eyes stared past me at nothing. I experienced it, night after night, jerking awake in a sweat to check Morgan was really passed out from exhaustion rather than dead, and then to toss and turn until morning.

There in the darkness with the clock ticking so slowly it could be running backwards, I faced some long-ignored things about myself.

Like the fact that I hadn't seen Pop or Pete since Steve's funeral years ago. That their voices were still in my head and that was fucked up.

Get up off the floor. You gotta be able to take more than one punch. Consider it a favor we're teaching you to be a man.

I could wrap my hand all the way around your scrawny arm. You sure you're an Ivers? Pop, I think your third son was kidnapped and swapped with a fucking fairy.

My brothers had been relentless, and I never really understood what it was about me that made them hate me so much or single me out the way they did. But my father's words had hurt the worst.

You're fucking useless.
You ain't got a lick of sense.

What good are those blue eyes and that blond hair of yours if you can't be a real man and use 'em to get the girls? What's wrong with you?

Thing was, girls have always liked me. Had whispered I was cute and stared at me back in school, even though I hadn't been all beefed up like I was now. I'd had plenty of offers to sleep with them. But I'd stayed away because, even though my brothers' words had taunted me to prove myself, I'd intuitively known they'd hate me more for it.

I'd admired the guys who'd seemed not to have a care in the world, wanting to be like them, and I'd avoided everybody.

After my dad had kicked me out, I'd lived on the streets, eating out of dumpsters until one day I'd heard a street kid talking about a way to make a lot of money. I'd questioned him, then shown up at the clubhouse. Blaze, eighteen and just taking over for his brother, had taken me under his wing. When I wasn't messing with cars, I was working out in the weight room. I'd dropped out of school, and Blaze had made me study for the GED. If it hadn't been for him, I was sure I'd be dead by now, or maybe worse, because if there was anything I'd learned on the streets, it was that some fates were worse than death.

For another week after the shooting, I continued escorting Morgan to his long-ass rehearsals where he didn't rehearse, just watched intensely, and his classes where he danced until he was slick with sweat and breathing hard. And I continued studying him, memorizing every expression that crossed his face. His high cheekbones, full lips, and expressive eyes captivated me, and I'd quit asking myself why. Scared I was letting him distract me too much, I renewed my efforts to watch the exits. I'd learned the face of every person who was supposed to be around and kept a watch for those who weren't.

The list of people wanting me to fix their cars was growing, but I never had any time. Several of the guys offered to take a day or two watching Morgan for me, but I didn't trust the kid in anyone else's care, and besides, there was my cover to consider. I was supposed to be a reporter doing a story on Morgan. Why would someone else show up in my place? Anyway, I knew the layout of the building, knew the corps de ballet's schedule, and I knew Morgan. I would take care of him.

Saturday came around, and I once again thanked God the fucking masochist ballet company let the dancers have Sunday off. I planned to spend mine sleeping, unless Morgan got other ideas. The kid looked exhausted, so I doubted it. Halfway through the day, the big guy, chief of the ballet or something, announced some chick named Katie had had to leave and called Morgan in to dance her part during rehearsal. My gut twisted. How was the kid supposed to dance a part he'd only watched a few times, and a female part at that?

But Morgan did it. He filled in for the girl like he'd been dancing the part himself every day since he got there, and I was in awe. I could tell the chief guy was impressed, too, or at least satisfied. I got the feeling he'd been testing Morgan, otherwise why the fuck hadn't he asked one of the female apprentices to fill in? At the end of the night, like a proud daddy, I tossed Morgan a candy bar from the machine in the hall.

Morgan looked at the Hershey bar like he didn't know what to do with it.

"For doing so great at the spur of the moment," I told him. A smile lit up his tired face that made the embarrassing moment worth it, and he unwrapped the candy bar. He broke it down the middle and handed half to me.

"For putting up with all this," Morgan said. Our eyes met. The whole thing felt so goddamn cheesy, I grumbled and didn't speak again until we were pulling out of the Arts Center.

I hated the scared look Morgan had every time we walked outside the building since the shooting. I wanted to rip Spoons's face off for putting it there, and I would if I got a chance.

"If it makes you feel any better, he ain't gonna try the same thing twice," I said to Morgan as he inched closer to me on the walk to the car.

He looked at me. "You mean he'll devise another way to kill me?"

"Well, yeah." We climbed in, and I headed for the Midtown Tunnel. I'd been changing up our route, even if it took longer to get home going a different way.

Morgan sank down in the seat and fiddled with the edge of his sweatshirt. "I can't go on like this. I'm so fucking stressed out."

"The way I see it, you ain't got much choice," I said. "You wanna be a dancer, so you gotta go to school. You wanna stay alive, so you gotta have me with you. Thing is, you gotta trust I'll take care of you and *relax.*"

Morgan brought up his knees to his chin, face broody. He was like a fucking bendable toy. I bet he could put both feet behind his head.

"It's gonna be okay, kid," I said. "I got you. Concentrate on spinning around and looking pretty."

Morgan groaned. "Shut up."

I laughed, feeling suddenly light.

Blaze met us at the door, and my stomach dropped. What had happened now? Morgan got that look again like he was going to throw up.

"What's going on?" I asked.

"Spoons got picked up for possession." Blaze followed us inside. The tension ran out of me in a flood.

Morgan looked at Blaze. "What? You mean, he's in jail?"

"For the time being," Blaze said.

"What does that mean for me?"

"Just a slight reprieve, since Spoons is the one with the beef against Jake, he's gonna be the one to want to settle things. So, if he's unavailable, that should mean you're safe for now."

"But don't go getting ideas," I said. "Spoons is likely to be out in a few days, plus nothing's stopping his guys from picking you up and keeping you until he gets out," I said.

Morgan deflated.

Blaze put an arm around Morgan's shoulders. "Tony's been working on it. He thinks he's got something. Give it a few more days."

After a long shower, I slipped on my shorts and headed for bed. Somehow, I'd gotten used to sleeping in the trundle again. Beside Morgan. It was nothing like sleeping next to Jake. Jake snored, for one thing. For another, I hadn't been aware of the guy like I was of his brother. Every rustle of the goddamn sheet had me thinking about parts of Morgan's body.

"You really think Spoons will get out?" Morgan asked from the darkness.

"Yeah. He always does. Probably has connections on the police force."

Morgan sighed. "Maybe I'd be better off with police protection."

I sat up. "Didn't you hear what I just said? The Pistons have got people on their side there. You couldn't be sure you wouldn't be delivered right to their front door."

"But... the police should be on my side!"

"Yeah, well, life's unfair."

Morgan was quiet for a while and then surprised me by saying, "Zeke, I'm scared."

I wasn't sure what to say to that, but I knew I didn't want Morgan to be afraid.

"I told you to trust me. I'm not gonna let anything happen to you. You believe me, don't you?" I waited, unsure if Morgan had the faith in me I wanted him to.

His answer came soft and low and turned my insides to butter. "Yeah, I believe you."

My chest tightened. "Good. Now, go to sleep."

I knew I'd be awake for a while.

⊛

I've learned the hard way it's when you least expect it that something bad happens. I should've expected it, but even with my promise to Morgan to keep him safe, long days of rehearsals with nothing happening made me complacent. It had been a long morning and Erik, the rehearsal coordinator, was in a snit. He called a break, and I was wondering if I could possibly get away for a smoke outside the back door when I noticed Morgan wasn't around. That's when Jon—the ginger Morgan talked to all the time—came running into the theater from the hall, face white as a sheet. I grabbed him by the shoulders.

"Where's Morgan?"

As I was supposed to be a reporter doing a story, that had to have seemed weird, but Jon was too shaken up to notice, and I didn't give a flying fuck what anybody thought at that point.

"We were in the restroom. Somebody—"

I didn't wait for him to finish but raced into the hallway and through the doors to the men's room, shoving open every stall, the sight of multiple drops of blood on the beige linoleum turning my guts to water. I rushed back out, past the crowd of dancers gathering in the lobby, and ran out the nearest exit.

For a few terrifying seconds, I turned under the large lights, not knowing which direction to go. No movement in the lines of cars parked out front. I headed for the back lot. That's when I heard muffled yelling and ran between the buildings. Two hefty dudes wearing Pistons cuts had Morgan between them, undoubtedly trying to get him to their ride in the back, but the kid was fighting like a hellcat.

Never pausing, I threw myself at his assailants, slamming one into the brick wall and kicking away his gun before turning to the other. Morgan managed to knee his captor in the balls, causing the guy to drop his blade. The bastard's face went green, but he hung onto the kid. Then Morgan sank to the ground like a sack of dead fish, making it impossible to move him and giving me the opening I needed.

As I crushed the bastard's nose with my fist, I was aware of the guy I'd hit first rolling over and trying to get to his feet. He had a scar running from his lip all the way to his hairline. I swiped the guy's piece off the ground and pointed it at the both of them.

"Might as well hand him over," the one with the scar said. "Save us all the time and trouble."

I pointed the gun at the guy's groin. "I'm giving you one chance to get out of here before I blow your nuts clean off your body."

A brief look passed between them, and they must have decided I was serious, because they backed up and ran.

I stuffed the gun between my jeans and the small of my back and bent over Morgan.

"You okay?"

Face ashen, Morgan stared, unseeing, pupils blending into dark irises. When I tried to help him up, he fought me, twisting and kicking at me just as he'd done with the Pistons creeps. He landed a few good blows, but I wrapped my arms around him and held on, talking softly in his ear.

"Come on, kid. It's me. It's only me. They're gone. You're safe. I told you I'd keep you safe."

The way all the fight ran out of him and he melted into me made me want to do something crazy, like plant kisses on his face. He was shaking, and I molded myself to him, absorbing his terror until it began to fade, and he buried his face in my chest.

A crowd surrounded us, but I didn't let go of Morgan.

"What happened?" Erik had his cell phone in his hand like he was ready to call 911. That couldn't happen.

"Guys ran off. I'm taking him down to the station," I said as I turned Morgan and wrapped my arm around him, leading him to the parking lot.

Of course, I had no intention of going to the cops. As soon as I'd driven a respectable distance from the Arts Center, I pulled over, got out, and opened the passenger door where Morgan sat stiff as a board. I pulled some tissues out of the glove compartment and dabbed at the cut on Morgan's lower lip.

"How're you doing?"

Morgan slowly shook his head. "I-I'm sorry. I didn't think there was any harm going to the restroom without you. I guess I never really believed they'd try anything inside the building, and Jon was with me."

"Yeah, fat lot of good the ginger did you. Pistons must've been camped out somewhere, waiting for their chance." Fuck, I didn't like thinking what they would've done to the kid. With Spoons in lock-up, they might have tortured Morgan for days.

Morgan's eyes flickered over my face. "Are you okay?"

I frowned. "Yeah. I'm fine."

Morgan ran his thumb along my cheek. "You're bleeding."

I wiped at it. "Just a scrape." I handed him a tissue, and he clenched it in his fist, brows lowering in an angry scowl.

"I've worked my whole life to get where I am right now. This is my one chance. If the company doesn't offer me a contract, I'll be fucked. I'm not going to let some thugs ruin it for me."

The adrenaline that had kept me cool under pressure had dissipated, all the terror I'd experienced when I'd realized Morgan was missing rising up in a swell of anger. I stood and slammed my fist on top of the car, making Morgan jump in his seat.

"Forget about dancing for now. Staying alive is what's goddamn important."

Morgan pushed past me and got out of the car. "Not if I can't do what I want to do with the rest of my life." He started to walk away, but I grabbed him by the arm.

"You won't have a life if they get hold of you again. Get back in the car. I don't know if it's safe here."

I'd been careful to make sure no one followed us, but I wasn't taking any chances.

Morgan glanced around nervously before climbing back in the SUV. I could see the kid was barely holding it together, and I felt kind of bad for scaring him all over again.

"Take me to a hotel," he said when I'd buckled my seat belt and started the car.

I looked at him. "What? Why?"

His voice shook. "I don't want to go to the clubhouse. Just... take me to a hotel. Any hotel. I've got my credit card. Please, Zeke."

Gritting my teeth at the way I felt when he looked at me like that, I pulled away from the curb. At the theater, when I'd realized he was gone—and then saw the blood on the bathroom floor—I'd imagined the fucking worst. I didn't know what Morgan Wentworth meant to me, but I couldn't deny he meant a lot.

"Don't be mad," he surprised me by saying.

"I'm not mad at you. And I'm not leaving you at a hotel."

"Good. Stay with me."

I grew hot at his words. I'd been sleeping in the same room as Morgan a while now, but imagining being in a hotel room with him did things to me. Things that scared the hell out of me.

Even so, I drove to the nearest Marriott and checked us in. The concierge didn't blink at two men getting a room together, and I was honestly too wired to care too much if he did. I'd already done more than I thought I'd ever do, like holding Morgan in my arms in public. We took the elevator to the fifth floor and walked down the hall.

"I'm taking a bath," Morgan announced as soon as we were in our room, and he disappeared into the john, leaving me alone. I closed the drapes and kicked off my shoes before calling Blaze, telling him what had happened and that we were spending the night at the Marriott.

"Probably for the best," Blaze said. "Tell Morgan it won't be long. Tony's got something."

"What is it?" I asked.

"I'll know more tomorrow. See you then, and be careful."

The following day was Sunday, thank Christ. No classes, no rehearsals. Morgan's schedule was fucking brutal. Being with him every day, seeing all those dancers putting everything they had into their art, had shown me how serious the competition was. Although I wished he'd take his safety more seriously, I felt for the kid and his dreams. Kind of made me think about my own. I liked working on cars, but where was I going with it?

The water stopped running in the tub. I could hear the occasional splash and couldn't help picturing Morgan in there naked and wet. I squeezed my cock beneath my zipper and turned on the TV before settling on one of the two queen-sized beds.

"You okay in there?" I called at the next commercial break.

No answer.

I got up and tried the bathroom door. It wasn't locked, and I eased it open. Morgan sat in the tub, eyes clenched shut, a washcloth stuffed against his mouth muffling his sobs.

I was way out of my depth, but I wasn't going to leave the kid crying alone in the tub. He was young, scared, and pretty out of his depth, too. I grabbed a towel off the rack.

"C'mere."

Morgan allowed me to lift him and wrap the big towel around his shoulders. The water had gone cold, and he was shivering. It hurt my heart, him hiding in there like I would've made fun of him for crying or something. I guided him into the main room and stood near the bed, arms encircling him. I'd found I liked how he felt against me. I didn't know what that meant, but there it was.

"It's okay to cry," I said into his hair.

"I'm not crying."

"Okay. You ain't crying."

Morgan looked up at me, dark eyes red-rimmed, brow furrowed, and lips tantalizingly plump and inviting. "I'm not."

"Okay."

Morgan huffed and leaned his cheek against my chest.

I might have tried to tell myself it was a brotherly thing I was feeling, except I was painfully aware of Morgan's nakedness under the towel and every point our bodies touched. My heart raced madly, and my dick was rock hard. I couldn't deny how much I wanted him, but that wasn't why I was holding him, and I didn't want him to think it was.

His breath fell hot on my now-damp T-shirt, and he clutched at the back of it. His voice came muffled from my shirt. "Thank you for saving me from those guys."

I ran my hand along his back to cup his neck. "You were holding your own. Nice move, going limp. Who taught you to do that?"

"I saw it on a talk show." Morgan pulled back, and I had to stop myself from drawing him close again. I almost swallowed my tongue when he shrugged off the towel.

"Morgan." The word came out rough. God, I wanted... something. I didn't even know exactly what. What did two men do together?

His cock was as long and lean as he was, and it stood out from his body. I couldn't stop looking at it.

Faggot. My father's voice echoed in my head.

"Fuck, Morgan."

His fingers trailed down my arm.

"Wanting me isn't a bad thing," he said softly.

"You're a *guy*."

"So?" He wrapped his arms around my neck. I was a goner. I knew it. Once my hands touched his bare skin, there was no going back. Our faces were so close...

I crossed the space, slamming our mouths together with a hungry intensity I'd never experienced before in my life. I couldn't get enough. Morgan gave it back just as rough, sucking and licking at my lips until I moaned and pushed my hard cock against his abdomen. God, he felt so smooth, so good under my hands. I gripped his ass, and his strangled cry set me on fire.

Morgan unzipped my jeans. I thought I would explode when his long fingers wrapped around my hard length.

"Take off your clothes," he said and I reached behind my back and tugged my shirt over my head. I tossed it aside.

My jeans and underwear were next. I couldn't wait to be naked and touching him. When I straightened, Morgan stepped forward, pressing his warm, sweet-smelling skin against mine, and I lifted him up into my arms. He wrapped his long legs around my waist, clinging to me while we kissed, his cock a solid pressure below my ribcage.

We toppled onto the bed.

I had absolutely no idea what I was doing. I'd never been with a man, only knew what I liked done to me. So I sucked each of Morgan's little brown nipples, not at all bothered by the fact he had hard pecs instead of soft, jiggling breasts. He whimpered, pulling at my hair. When my dripping cock brushed Morgan's, pleasure darted through me.

"I want to suck you," Morgan said, and I let out a tortured groan. There was no going back from this.

I didn't want to.

I straightened and stood at the foot of the bed, and Morgan scooted down so his legs dangled off it. I thought I'd lose it when he balanced the head of my cock on his tongue and then toyed with my studded piercing. I groaned when he sucked me in. I'd gone to heaven. The clouds opened up and the voices of the heavenly choir sang out.

Fuck, Morgan's mouth was better than any chick's. He knew how to please me, and I wondered how many Italian guys he'd sucked back in Milan. The thought infuriated me. When his head started bobbing, I almost blew, but Morgan's fingers wrapped around my nuts and tugged, staving off my orgasm.

Wet, pink lips worked over my dick until I tensed again, only to have the little tease let go and begin licking up and down my shaft. His enthusiasm ratcheted up my desire yet another notch. *Fuck, he was sexy.*

"You taste so good," he said before tonguing the underside of my aching nuts.

I was barely coherent in my reply, which sounded something like, "*Mmhm...uuh-nt.*"

Morgan slid his hand up to tease the trail of hair running from my navel to my cock. He tugged at it roughly while slurping on my sensitive head.

Somewhere in my fog of lust, I realized I wasn't freaking over a guy sucking me. Because it was Morgan—the person I'd been intensely focused on every day for the past two weeks, and if I was being honest with myself, the person I'd wanted from the moment he'd turned and lobbed a banana in my face.

Releasing my cock, Morgan caught his breath before catching the precum from the tip with his tongue. *So fucking hot.*

He bit his bottom lip and looked up at me with those chocolate-colored eyes. "I want you to fuck me," he said, and my cock jerked. If he hadn't been squeezing the base, I would have shot in his face. *God, what an image.*

"Will you?" he asked.

Unable to form words, I nodded jerkily.

"Do you have a condom?" Morgan asked.

I almost fell trying to get to it. Morgan disappeared into the bathroom and came back with a small bottle of hotel lotion. I squeezed my aching dick as I watched him finger himself open, glad I'd beaten one off that morning in the shower, or else I know I would have exploded by then. Thinking about where my cock was going had me shaking.

I'd never given much thought about the logistics of two men doing it. The way my old man and brothers were, I spent most of my time making sure I never thought about men at all.

"It's lubricated," I said, holding up the condom.

"Go easy." Morgan turned over on the bed, and I stared, forgetting everything except those two gorgeous, golden globes. Perfectly round and smooth, they rose invitingly from the dip of Morgan's back. Morgan reached back and pulled them open, revealing the wet star between.

I moaned. I'd never fucked a woman's ass — it was too much like, well, what I was about to do.

"I don't know what I'm doing," I croaked even as I moved closer.

Morgan let go of his ass cheeks and eased onto his stomach sliding up one knee. "Just...go really slow."

Looking at the expanse of olive skin below me, I couldn't decide what I wanted to touch first. Bending, I ran my tongue along Morgan's smooth shoulder, loving the breathy noise he made, like he was surprised I hadn't just crammed my dick into his ass and gotten on with it. I continued down the curve of his back, stopping at the two divots above his butt. The sudden urge to bury my face between his ass cheeks shocked me. I'd never done that kind of thing before. Overwhelmed, I settled for nipping at the soft globes before covering Morgan's body with mine. He spread his legs as my cock nudged at him. Face buried in Morgan's neck, I pushed the head of my cock inside the tiny hole.

Morgan gasped and stiffened. "Stop. Wait just a second."

I froze, watching Morgan's profile. He lay breathing deeply through his nose, and just when it got to the point I was ready to pull back out, he finally began to relax, loosening around me.

"Okay. Keep going." Morgan pushed back and clenched, the rim of his ass grasping at the head of my cock. Pleasure blasted through my body. I continued to slowly ease inside, the feeling of my cock being eaten up by that tiny hole overwhelming everything else. I even forgot to breathe.

"God, Zeke. *Oh, God...*" Morgan's face had become blissful. He clutched at the pillow and wiggled beneath me, sending pure nirvana through my body.

Now I was the one begging him to stop. "Give me a minute, or this will be over way too soon."

Morgan stilled, and the grip his body had on my cock eased as he relaxed into the mattress.

"I feel so full," he said. "So good."

The fact I had my dick up a dude's ass should have been a monumental turn-off, but it was *Morgan*, and I was harder than fuck.

When I could move again without shooting off, I pushed up on my arms and looked between us to where my blond pubes brushed against the swell of Morgan's ass. Christ, how was I going to get through this without embarrassing myself? We were both trembling and breathing hard, and we hadn't even really started yet. I silently counted to twenty, blanking out my mind, before giving the first shallow thrust. And then another.

Morgan buried his face in the pillow and moaned.

The sight of my cock moving in and out of his ass was the fucking hottest thing I'd ever seen, and I had to concentrate hard not to fly over the edge. Soon, though, the smell of sweat and Morgan's moans undid me, and I sped up until loud slapping noises overcame the sounds of our harsh breathing.

After a few minutes, Morgan struggled to his knees, and I thrust harder, loving the way he white-knuckled the sheets and called out my name; how his ass sucked me in; how he spread his legs wider and tilted up to meet my every stroke. I fucked him hard, holding off as long as I could, white filling my vision as our balls smacked together. An inhuman sound rose from my chest, tearing out of my throat like a war cry.

Morgan tensed, convulsing beneath me, ass a tight mouth gripping my cock. I sucked in air, eyes rolling back as I shot my load into the condom, wishing I was coating his insides.

I was so turned on, I didn't soften much, so I kept going, slowing my pace a little, hoping to pull more of the sweet sounds from Morgan's lips.

Sweat dripped into my eyes. I couldn't quite hit the pinnacle again, but Morgan whimpered and bucked, so I reached beneath him and tugged on his slick cock like I would my own until he came a second time like the fucking teenager he was. Then I eased out and took care of the condom.

After a moment, Morgan rolled to face me and pulled the sheet over us. Our eyes locked. It was like a sappy movie, but I didn't care. I felt god-damned sappy after that.

"Thank you," he said.

I squirmed. "You don't gotta thank me."

He rolled my nipple between his thumb and forefinger. "Are you going to have an existential crisis now?"

"Not tonight," I said, and pulled him closer. "God, I thought you were gonna squeeze my fucking cock in half. Is it always that good?" So, maybe I was fishing a little.

Morgan shook his head and buried his face in my armpit. I could feel him smiling against my skin. The air conditioner kicked on, and we just lay there, holding each other.

CHAPTER EIGHT

Morgan

Zeke fell asleep, but I couldn't. I lay listening to his soft breathing and the sound of the air conditioner turning on and off at intervals. Face wiped of all thought, Zeke looked peaceful, and I wanted to kiss him.

He'd fucked me. My first time. Of course, Zeke hadn't known he'd taken my virginity, and I didn't want him to ever know it. It had had to be him, that's all. I'd realized it the moment he'd pulled me out of the tub and held me. Or maybe before that, I don't know. After what happened at the theater, I'd wanted to be alone. But with Zeke there. Alone with him.

I hoped he wouldn't regret what we'd done.

I sighed. Zeke had a big, thick cock, and it had hurt, but he'd gone slow, and I'd adjusted. When his Prince Albert had skidded against my prostate, I'd thought I was going to turn inside out with pleasure. Of course the man would have a cock piercing. I'd almost shot off when I saw it. Sucking him had been *amazing*. Just remembering got me half-hard again.

I snuggled closer to Zeke, the light fur on his chest tickling my nose. The cologne he'd put on that morning still lingered, along with the vague scent of his last cigarette. The no-smoking rule in the theater had forced him to cut down, and he didn't smoke around me because I gave him grief about it. I'd like to think he'd quit altogether, but I was sure after I was gone he'd go back to it with a vengeance.

The sex had helped settle the panic I'd thought would consume me after the attack. Nothing like two mega orgasms to reset a guy's power switch. Three huge guys had just appeared in the theater restroom, and there had been nothing I could do to get away. I'd somehow imagined I would be more capable in a situation like that, but one had popped me in the face, then the trio had plucked me up like I'd weighed nothing and carried me out of the building. The one guy's hand over my mouth had blocked my nostrils, and if it hadn't caused me to black out, they might not have stopped in the alley like they did, giving Zeke time to get to me. The thought sent chills down my spine. I shivered, and Zeke's arm tightened around me in sleep.

As soon as I'd come to, I'd started kicking and yelling. The guy had covered my mouth again, but thankfully that time I'd been able to breathe. I'd never been so relieved as when Zeke had come barreling around the corner.

Not wanting to think about the attack anymore, I burrowed deeper into Zeke's arms, pressing my nose to his skin.

My ass was sore. Zeke was a powerhouse and had fucked me to within an inch of my life, which in all fairness, I'd asked for. *Begged for*, more like. I smiled into the pillow thinking about it.

A faint buzzing had me rolling out of bed and looking around the room for my cell phone. Zeke slept on, so I closed myself in the bathroom and answered.

"Hello?"

"Hey, Morgan, this is Jon. You okay?" I could hear the clamor of rehearsal letting up in the background.

"Yeah... I'm fine, thanks." I suppressed a yelp as I sat down on the cold toilet seat.

"Did you file a police report?"

No way the Hedonists wanted club business to reach the police unless it had to. I knew from Jake that even though the club was on the total up-and-up, they tried to stay under the radar of the local police, who weren't above harassing them just because they could. But Jon and everyone else would be expecting me to file a report.

"All taken care of."

"Sorry to bother you tonight. I'm sure you're exhausted. I was just worried."

"That's okay. I appreciate it."

"Who were those guys?"

"No idea. The police think they were after my family's money."

Jon made a noise like a shudder ran through him. "God, that's awful. Hope they catch them."

"Me, too. I'll see you Monday, okay?"

"Yeah, okay."

When I got back in the bedroom, Zeke was awake, baby blue eyes taking in my nakedness in a way that made my cheeks flame and my cock jump.

"C'mere," he said, lifting up the sheet, and I did without hesitation.

I settled against him, chest to chest, cock to cock. I'd expected Zeke to freak about what we'd done, but he seemed fine. His lips moved over mine in a hungry, demanding dance. Our tongues touched, and my cock moved against his. *God, he was going to incinerate me.*

I couldn't regret any of it. I'd needed it. Maybe Zeke had, too. And the hotel room felt like some kind of magical bubble—a time and place away from everyone else. As I kissed him deeply, I began moving against him. Zeke moaned into my mouth and rolled so he was on his back with me on top, bending his knees so he could grind our cocks together. The combination of his mouth on mine, his palms squeezing my ass, and our cocks sliding against one another sent tremors rocking through my body.

Fuck, it felt so good. Our gasps and groans soon tore our mouths apart, and I pressed my forehead to his as we barreled toward release, breathing hard, bodies jerking and eyes locked as our cocks shot between us within seconds of each other.

"Holy shit," Zeke murmured as I sagged against him. I sighed contentedly when he began stroking my hair.

I smiled a little giddily. "Yeah, me, too. And then some."

"What the hell was that we just did?"

"I think it's called *frottage.*"

Zeke grunted. "Whatever it was, it felt insanely good."

I sank into sleep, and the next thing I knew, pearly pink light shone from between the heavy drapes. I'd rolled off Zeke, and he spooned against me, arm draped over my middle. I didn't ever want to move.

"Blaze said Tony found something," Zeke said when he realized I was awake.

I looked over my shoulder at him. "What?"

"He didn't tell me. We'll find out when we get home."

Home. The clubhouse wasn't my home, and sadness suddenly enveloped me.

"Where's your family?" I asked, tracing the muscles along Zeke's arm. I knew I was pushing since he'd made it pretty clear last time he didn't want to talk about it, but I wanted to know the man I'd given myself to, even if we never went any further than that.

He tensed against me.

"I told you, the club's my family."

"What about your parents?"

Zeke sighed. I thought he'd tell me to mind my own business, but he surprised me by answering. "Ma's dead, my brother who was a cop is dead. My pop might as well be, 'cause I haven't talked to him in years. My other brother Pete got married and moved away, I think."

"You think?"

"We weren't what you'd call close."

"I'm sorry." I kissed his arm. In some ways, the gesture felt more intimate than what we'd done the night before, crazy as that sounded, and I thought Zeke might pull away, but he stayed put.

"No reason to be," he said.

"I know what it's like to be alone."

"We both got friends," Zeke said.

"Yeah, I guess." I had Nikki, and now I had Jon and some of the others at Manhattan ballet. And I had Harvey and the guys in the club. The holidays would be hard. I'd thought Jake and I would be spending them together. I'd had so many plans.

Zeke ran his hand over my bare chest, and tingles skated down my spine. "I'm sorry, kid," he said, as though he'd read my mind.

"So, you've lost a brother, too."

Zeke was quiet for a moment. When he spoke, he sounded regretful. "I guess that was part of why I was so hard on you the day we met."

"You mean when you kicked my ass all over Nikki's apartment?"

"I didn't kick your ass."

I laughed. "Maybe not, but you gave me a few bruises. I thought you were some kind of crazy rapist or something."

Zeke's chuckle rumbled against my back. He smoothed down my hair with his hand. "Sorry, kid. The whole thing with Jake made me think of Steve, I guess. We were never close, but now we never will be, you know?"

I nodded, sadness drifting over me like a dark cloud.

Missing Jake had been part of the reason I'd been crying in the bathtub the night before. After the shock of the attack, the fact I had no one had crashed into me like a freight train. And then Zeke had held me. I sighed and relaxed against him, and we dozed for a while.

Eventually, we had to leave our bubble. We got up and dressed, and Zeke checked us out. I stayed close to him, eyes darting everywhere, feeling like any minute someone would jump out of hiding and grab me. I wondered what Blaze might have found out and if whatever it was would really keep the rival gang away.

We picked up some coffee and croissants at a nearby drive-thru and headed for the clubhouse. I waited for things to get awkward between us, but they didn't. Amazingly, Zeke seemed okay with what we'd done. He didn't avoid my eyes or jerk away from my touch, and I was glad. Maybe I'd misjudged him, and he wasn't as closeted as I'd thought. I didn't fool myself into thinking there would be anything between us, but I was happy what we'd done hadn't spoiled our newfound friendship.

Blaze met us at the door.

"Everything okay?"

I nodded. "Fine."

He wrapped his arm around my shoulder and led me inside. "I'm sorry about all this, Morgan, but you'll be glad to know it's over."

I stopped in the middle of the living room and faced Blaze. "Zeke said you found out something..." I bit my lip nervously and waited.

"Tony heard from a friend of a friend on the police force who received information last June from the Pistons about a rival group, the Hogs. The intel sent five of the Hogs, including their president, to prison for life. The Hogs are even worse than the Pistons—one-percenters who don't fool around. If they were to find out who'd squealed, they'd slaughter the Pistons without thinking twice. Blow up their clubhouse, make their families pay, too. A short visit with Spoons at the jail was all it took. He looked like he was gonna throw up the slop they serve there. The Pistons aren't gonna pursue you." Blaze's grin was huge.

It couldn't be that easy. Could it?

"But... just like that? Couldn't he be lying about leaving me alone?"

"He's not lying. I made sure Spoons knew every single one of us and some others besides are sitting on this information. If he so much as looks at you funny, they're dead. The Hogs have come back tougher than ever with a new president who'd sooner cut a guy's balls off than hear what he had to say."

My eyes went to Zeke. He nodded.

"Okay, well, I guess if you think it's okay, it must be."

Blaze squeezed my shoulder. "It is. I promise. Now you can relax and get on with your life. But I hope you won't be a stranger."

I think we all knew our future paths were unlikely to cross, but I smiled and said, "Of course."

I headed for the bedroom and a quick internet search of one-percenters told me the Hogs were of the outlaw variety and enjoyed using deadly force, which was why Spoons was afraid of them.

I got my duffel bag out of the closet and began packing.

Swish appeared in the doorway, a very small dog in his arms.

"It's so cute." I couldn't help going over to pet it. "What kind is it?"

"She's a teacup poodle. I just got her fixed up and ready for her owners."

"Aw." I brought the little dog to my face and nuzzled it. She was an apricot color and the cutest thing I'd ever seen. Swish had put a tiny pink bow in her hair. Reluctantly, I handed her back to Swish.

"Good news, huh?" he asked as I resumed packing.

I nodded. Relief at being out of danger warred with an aching disappointment about leaving Zeke.

Still glad you slept with him? I asked myself. I had to admit I was.

When I finished packing, I sat on the edge of the bed. "What kind of film business is the club in, exactly?"

Swish looked up from adjusting the dog's rhinestone collar. "You don't know? Blaze runs a legit porn company. Hard Time Productions."

"I figured it was something like that." It fit with the bits and pieces of things I'd heard over the few weeks I'd been staying there.

"Does, uh, Zeke do it? Work in the business?" Zeke was certainly fit enough, but I hated the thought of him fucking women, especially for the camera.

"Naw. He just works on cars. But Hung's a fan favorite," Swish said.

"Oh, my God." I thought of something. "Jake did it?"

"He didn't act, he filmed. Vanessa, the girl he took up with, was a popular star. She had no gag reflex whatsoever."

I stood, putting my duffel over my shoulder, and grabbed my back-pack.

Swish side-hugged me. "I'm gonna miss you."

"Me, too. Come see me when I get my own place."

An idea had been forming in the back of my mind since Blaze had told me I was free. I no longer wanted to stay at the academy dorms. I wanted to get my own apartment. Make it a home.

Standing, I braced myself for the rest of my goodbyes. Zeke was going to be the hardest, and I couldn't do it like I wanted to with everyone around. I shouldered my bag and walked into the living room.

I needn't have worried; Zeke was nowhere to be found.

CHAPTER NINE

Morgan

The next couple months were crazy busy for me. I managed to find a small apartment close enough to walk to the Arts Center, but I didn't have time to do anything but order a couch and bed and take care of a few minor things before rehearsals started up for *The Nutcracker*. The apprentices were required to dance all fifty-two performances, which only counted as one of the eight productions we had to do, and I found myself without a moment to breathe.

At first, there'd been questions about what had happened to Zeke. I'd told everyone he'd decided to wrap up the article after the attack, and thankfully no one asked when the article would be published. Undoubtedly all they had time for after long days of rehearsal was to face-plant in bed, sleep like the dead, and wake up at dawn to start all over again.

I didn't think things could get any crazier, but a few rehearsals into *The Nutcracker*, the male principal twisted his back, and I was suddenly promoted from one of the mice to the role of the prince. For weeks, I didn't know if I was coming or going, dancing even in my sleep, the voice of the choreographer ringing through my dreams every night — *up, up, UP! – low arm, high arm, low arm, high arm! –* an echo of the grueling hours spent under his direction. I hurt *everywhere*.

But the craziness got me through the holidays. Christmas consisted of a short, catered party at the end of a performance, and I found myself standing in the corner drinking punch and thinking of Zeke. I hadn't seen nor spoken to him since I'd left the clubhouse, and I missed him. On impulse, I typed out a Merry Christmas text and pushed send before I could chicken out.

I didn't get a reply.

Before I knew it, New Year's Eve arrived, always a big deal in New York City. We'd danced our final performance that afternoon, and I stood crammed among the riot of people gathered to watch the ball drop in Times Square, a few of my fellow apprentices with me. As the countdown began, I looked around for Nikki, but she'd disappeared into the crowd with her boyfriend-of-the-hour. I kept trying to convince her she should call Paul, who I'd really liked and thought was good for her, but she never listened.

Together with the rest of the crowd, I shouted, "3,2,1, Happy New Year!" and Jon surprised me by spinning me around into a kiss that was much more than a friendly peck.

I gently pushed him away and smiled before hugging Lyla and then Gage. When I turned back to Jon, he was hugging someone else, and for the next two hours, we pretended he'd never had his tongue down my throat.

When I got home, I kicked off my shoes and flopped down on the sofa. I swiped through my phone for a few minutes, unwinding from the events of the day. A text from Blaze telling me Happy New Year, and one from Swish and Dante each, but none from the person I really wanted to hear from.

I opened my email. Gerald Peters had sent a brief message about the next board meeting. I supposed it was time to make an appearance. I tapped out a quick reply that I would be there and stretched out, mind returning to Jon and the unexpected kiss. I liked him, but there was no real spark there. When I closed my eyes, I could still feel the steel ball in Zeke's tongue rubbing against mine.

My body still ached for him.

Maybe that's because he's the only man you've ever slept with, I told myself.

Maybe. But when I thought of sleeping with someone else, my ardor shut down.

My phone pinged and I lifted it from my lap to look at the screen.

Nikki: *Make it home safe?*

Me: *Yeah. You?*

Nikki: *Yeah. Sorry I lost you in the crowd. Can you have lunch with me tomorrow?*

I considered. I needed to take my dad's car somewhere to be looked over before I tried to sell it, but I probably wouldn't have enough time to do that over lunch. I must have taken too long to reply, because my phone pinged again.

Nikki: *Come on. We need to catch up.*

Me: *Lol, you don't have to pretend you have interesting news. I still want to see you.*

Nikki: *Asshole. Lunch or no?*

Me: *Sure. But it'll have to be someplace close to the Arts Center.*

Nikki: *I'll meet you out front. What time?*

We ironed out the details and disconnected. Too tired to move to the bed or even to undress, I pulled the afghan off the back of the couch and settled in. As was typical for my life, it only seemed seconds later when light peeked through the blinds.

Shit. Was I late? I practically fell off the couch trying to get untangled from the afghan.

I checked my phone. I had nineteen minutes to get to the theater. Why hadn't I set my alarm? I had to skip a shower, but since I'd had one before going to Times Square, I figured I'd be okay. I plugged up my phone to charge, went to the bathroom, brushed my teeth, slathered on deodorant, and tried to do something with my mess of curls. My hair had grown out considerably, but I'd had no time for a cut. Giving up, I pulled it back with an elastic band, slipped on a pair of shoes, and grabbed my coat and dance bag.

As per usual for January in New York, it was fucking freezing outside. I speed-walked down the sidewalk, dodging the occasional person huddled in their coat out walking their dog, my eyes on the top of the Arts Center several blocks up the street. Memories of the night before and Jon's kiss came to mind, and of course, I thought of Zeke. The way it felt when he'd held me. His hands on me. His lips.

Shit, I had to stop this. It was unlikely I would ever see Zeke again. Hell, he hadn't even bothered to text me back a simple Merry Christmas.

Maybe he's finally had that existential crisis, I thought sadly. I'd gotten the idea that Zeke's home life had been pretty bad, and I wouldn't be surprised if homophobia had been strong there.

The theater was warm, *thank fuck.* I unwrapped the red scarf from around my nose and mouth and shed my jacket, hanging it beside dozens of others in the back room before heading down the hall to the cloister of studios at the far end. Everyone was just finishing up his and her stretches and I got the evil eye from Erik, aka the principal voice in my dreams. Tossing my bag into a corner with several others, I hurried to the barre.

As always, the morning flew by. I was pouring sweat by the time I finished and had to wipe down in the bathroom before pulling on the extra clothes from my bag. I'd finished my second bottle of water by the time I arrived outside and spotted Nikki sitting on the edge of the fountain. I skipped down the stairs to meet her.

"You smell like baby wipes," she said as she hugged me.

"I tried to clean up."

"For me? Thanks. Didn't know you cared."

"I don't like to stink around anybody."

"And here I thought I was special."

We'd been walking fast toward Nikki's blue Nissan, gloved hands deep in the pockets of our coats, breath smoking in front of us. My nose tingled from the cold.

"Hey, where do you go to get your car tuned?" I asked as we slid inside, shivering until the heater warmed up. "I need to take Dad's BMW in. Selling it is at the top of my to-do list for the new year."

"Why don't you just get it towed? It's not like you need the money."

"It's a good car," I said. This is what bugged me about Nikki: she wasn't the greatest with money. Sure, she'd gone out on her own to earn a living, but I think always knowing she had family money to fall back on, she wasn't very savvy with it. Whereas, as the young CEO of a huge corporation, I was always aware of the responsibility I had for hundreds of livelihoods, even if I didn't take much part in running things.

"I'll text you the address." Nikki pulled out of the parking lot. "Did you have fun last night?"

I shrugged. "It was okay. How about you? What's all this stuff we need to catch up on? I can sum up my life in one word. Dance."

"As always," Nikki said. "It wasn't until I stopped dancing that I realized what little life I had. So I did something I've always wanted to do. I took up art classes at the community college near my apartment."

"What kind of art?"

"Painting. The first semester was watercolors, and we're about to start on oils. I really enjoy it."

Nikki talked about painting while circling the block looking for a parking space close to the deli where we'd planned to eat. She finally snagged one and parallel parked like a pro. I fed coins to the meter, and we rushed toward the warmth of the shop. Inside, we thawed out as we stood in the short line and perused the menu behind the counter. I ordered some hot tea with a turkey sandwich, and Nikki ordered vegetable soup. Once seated, I looked at her expectantly.

"Well?"

"Well, what?"

"We've reached the conclusion you're the only one with a life, so spill."

Nikki sighed. "I ran into Paul last night."

"At Times Square?"

"No, right after. I took a cab home, and he was waiting for me outside the building."

"What? In the cold?"

Nikki nodded. "He wants to get back together." Her fingers went to her lips, a soft look on her face. "He kissed me."

"I never understood why you broke up with him in the first place. You two were great together."

Nikki studied her napkin. "We were. Too good, I think."

"Huh?"

She shook her head. "It's dumb, I know, but I just wanted to end things before they ended by themselves."

I scrunched up my face. "What?"

"Good things always end. Always. I like to feel a little in control, you know?"

"Sounds like a line from a movie. A really bad one that doesn't make any sense."

"But it's true. Anything really good dies a terrible death."

"So, let me get this straight: you sabotaged your relationship just in case you might get hurt later on?"

"I didn't sabotage it. It's not like I plotted for him to walk in on me with someone else or something. That really would be a bad movie. I just decided it was time to move on."

"That's bullshit, Nik. I'd thought there had to be some hidden reason why you'd broken up with him, but not that things were too good."

Nikki looked down into her bowl.

I gently kicked her foot under the table. "You getting back together with him?"

Nikki began eating.

"Nik?"

She glanced at me. "I don't know, all right? I told him I'd call him."

I smiled. That was better than a hard no.

"Enough about me," Nikki said. "Who did you kiss at midnight?"

I took a sip of tea and set the Styrofoam cup on the table. "Jon kissed me."

"Jon, the cute ginger, Jon?"

I nodded.

Nikki smiled. "I didn't know he liked you."

"Neither did I."

"Was the kiss bad?"

"No, not at all. But it was unexpected and had a lot more tongue than I would have liked. I guess I just hadn't ever thought of Jon that way."

"You don't find him attractive?"

I shrugged. "Sure."

"It's Zeke, isn't it."

I looked up. "What?"

"Oh, come on, Morgan. I could see there was something going on between you. Behind the truce you'd declared was a whole lot of eye-fucking and tortured looks. You should have gotten it out of your system before you left."

I opened my mouth and shut it again. Nikki had become a frequent visitor to the clubhouse while I was there. She'd gotten to be pretty good friends with Blaze and a few times when Zeke and I had left in the morning, she'd be sleeping up on the couch. Had Zeke and I really been looking at each other like that? I concentrated on eating, and the silence drew out between us.

When I ventured what I hoped was a casual glance, Nikki was watching me.

"Morgan, did you and Zeke sleep together?"

When I didn't answer, she put down her spoon. "I was only kidding! You said he was straight."

"I said I was pretty sure he was in the closet."

She leaned forward. "What happened?"

"It's a long story."

"You'd better hurry up, then, because you're not going anywhere until I hear it."

By the time I'd told it all, we'd finished eating and were back in the car.

"I can't believe you had the guts," Nikki said, awed.

I pulled on my gloves. "Gee, thanks."

Shaking her head, Nikki eased from the curb into traffic. "I just mean... look. You've been locked away in Milan for so long—"

"I was hardly locked away."

Nikki gave me a look. "I know you, Morgan. Dance has always been your life. And I understand that. It was mine, too. Since my injury, I've discovered just how much. I've had to make a life outside of dance because I didn't have one before. I'll tell you a secret; as heartbroken as I was over my injury, I'm glad now that it happened."

That wasn't as difficult for me to imagine as she might think. More and more lately, I wanted a life outside of dance. But was it possible? And if it wasn't, did I still want to devote half my life to ballet?

Nikki pulled into the Arts Center parking lot. "What is it about Zeke that made you want to lose your virginity to him?" she asked.

"I lost my virginity to you."

"You know what I mean. Your gay virginity, which is more important, because you're gay. Plus, I know you're a bottom, and it's not like I pegged you or anything."

I snorted at the thought of Nikki wearing a strap-on.

"I really want to know what it is about him, Morgan. I'll admit he's hot, but he seems kind of... well, kind of a jerk." Her face fell. "Or is that what it is? You like that he's an ass."

"No. There's more to Zeke than what you see. I don't really know what it was that drew me to him." Just thinking about Zeke had my heart thumping faster.

I unbuckled my seatbelt and wound my scarf around my neck.

"The company okay?" Nikki asked.

Oh, I'd forgotten to tell her my biggest news. "Jon's brother wants to put an LGBTQ center in one of our buildings. I'm going to bring it up at the next board meeting."

Nikki smiled. "I'm glad you're going to use your position for good."

I grinned. "And not evil?" I climbed out of the car then leaned in. "Lunch was great. We'll have to try to do this more than once every couple of months."

"Definitely."

I waved and jogged up the steps to the building. Talking about Zeke had put me off balance. I wanted to see him—not to start anything up, just for a little closure. After all, I hadn't gotten to say goodbye to him, and I'd always wondered why he couldn't at least have given me a Merry Christmas in return. Maybe it was what I needed to put him out of my mind for good.

CHAPTER TEN

Morgan

The following night, I picked up the BMW from the garage. My plan was to have Zeke take a look at it. When I pulled up to the clubhouse, I climbed out and stood uncertainly in the yard. A few lights were still on inside, including the one in the garage. I knew Zeke worked late.

The air was bitter cold, and the sky spewed tiny white snowflakes. Nervously fiddling with my scarf, I resisted the urge to turn around and leave. This had sounded like a good idea in my head, but was it really? What if Zeke didn't want to see me? What if he saw through the thin excuse of having him look at my car?

Taking a deep breath, I screwed up my courage and headed up the front steps.

Dante answered my knock, looking like he'd just rolled off the couch, his long hair in a tangle and eyes squinting in the porch light.

"Morgan, hi." He coughed hoarsely into his hand.

"Did I wake you up?"

"What? No. Well, maybe I fell asleep in front of the TV. Got a cold. Good to see you, man."

Dante stood aside, and I walked into the warm foyer.

"What's up? I was beginning to think we'd never see you again."

"Sorry, my schedule's been really heavy."

"I heard you danced a principal part in *The Nutcracker*. Congratulations."

Surprised, I smiled. "How'd you know about that?"

Dante thought about it. "I'm pretty sure Zeke mentioned it."

Zeke? How did *he* know about it? "Speaking of Zeke, I wanted to talk to him. Is he around?"

"He's out in the garage." Dante grabbed some tissues from a box by the couch and blew his nose. "Everything going okay?"

I smiled. "Yeah. Just hectic."

I headed for the door to the garage.

Light from an uncovered bulb cast a glow around a black Toyota Camry with a couple of legs sticking out from beneath it. I recognized Zeke's beat-up sneakers.

"Zeke?"

A bang followed by a volley of cursing preceded Zeke sliding out from under the car on a rolling board. He blinked up at me, hand on his head, and my heart kicked into overdrive. I'd forgotten just how blue his eyes were.

"Morgan?" Zeke looked like he was seeing a ghost.

"Sorry, I startled you."

"What are you doing here?"

I chewed on my lip. "Um, well, I wanted to see if you could look at my car."

Zeke frowned. "You got a car?"

"My dad's. I want to sell it."

Zeke let out a breath and got to his feet.

I cleared my throat, feeling awkward. "I just need the car tuned or whatever before I advertise it."

Zeke's gaze roamed over me, lighting me up like the Vegas Strip at sunset. He hit the button to raise the garage door, which creaked loudly as it rolled up against the ceiling. As cold air hit my calves, then thighs, then the rest of me, I hunkered down in my heavy coat. The snow was picking up outside. Zeke wore only a tattered tank top and jeans but appeared oblivious to the frigid weather as he circled the BMW. I blushed, remembering the warmth that emanated from that powerhouse of a body.

"When do you need it?" Zeke asked.

Down the street, a trashcan rattled and a cat yowled. My nose stung. I blinked the snowflakes from my eyelashes.

"It doesn't really matter. I'm tired of paying to have it stored and want to sell it as soon as possible. It's been idle for a couple years but seems to drive well." I held out the key.

When Zeke took it, my skin tingled where our hands touched. I wanted to grab him up and kiss him.

I'd been a fool to think seeing Zeke again would give me closure. I wanted him more than ever.

I wondered if he ever even thought about that night in the hotel.

"I can get to it in the next few days," Zeke said.

I managed to keep my voice even. "Thanks. I'll pay whatever you charge, of course."

Zeke looked up at the sky. Snow already covered the hood of the car.

"How're you gonna get home?"

I pulled my cell phone out of my pocket. "I'll call an Uber."

"To Manhattan? It'll cost you a fortune."

I shrugged. "Maybe thirty-five dollars."

"They'll double the price to come out in this weather." I'd noticed before that Zeke and I had different ideas about what constituted a fortune, which made sense as everyone didn't come from money like I did. I was careful with mine but thought seventy dollars well worth a ride home in this weather; however, I didn't want to look like a rich dick.

"You're probably right," I said.

"Come on, I'll give you a ride."

My heart hammered. "Are you sure?"

Zeke stretched his back, and I couldn't pull my gaze from his rippling muscles.

"I need a break anyway. I'll just grab my jacket." He disappeared inside the house, and I stood staring out into the swirling snow, feeling like I was stepping off a cliff into the unknown.

He's just driving you home, I told myself. It's not like it's a fucking date or anything.

When Zeke returned, he motioned me to get into the SUV parked at the other end of the garage. For the first time, I noticed the line of bikes was gone.

"Where is everybody?"

"Rally this weekend in Pennsylvania," Zeke said. "Dante and I stayed behind. He's sick, and I've gotta catch up on work. Even Swish went. He rode bitch with Ax."

I wrinkled my nose at the term.

When we were both inside the car, I pulled a bill out of my wallet and held it out to Zeke. "At least let me pay for gas."

"Not necessary."

"Come on. It's only a third of what I'd be paying for an Uber."

"Christ. I know you won't shut up until I take it." Zeke pulled the bill from my hand and lifted in the seat enough to stuff it into his pocket.

"You're right, I won't."

He pulled out of the garage, and I relaxed into the seat.

After a few minutes of silence in which all I could think about was the man sitting beside me, Zeke glanced my way. "How come you brought the car to me? There have to be plenty of shops near you."

I had to see you again. "I'd rather take it to someone I know than to a stranger and thought you'd appreciate the business."

Zeke grunted.

"I've missed that about you," I said.

"What?"

"The grunting. You could carry on a whole conversation with them, just by changing the inflection."

Zeke huffed out a laugh. "You're crazy."

I smiled, enjoying just being with him again. "Anything new?" I asked after a moment.

"Not really."

"Did you get my text at Christmas?"

"Yeah. Thanks," he added.

The silence became awkward. Before I'd left, we'd gotten to the point where we'd talked almost nonstop when he drove me to and from the Arts Center, and when we weren't talking, the silence felt easy. Nothing like this. Had sleeping together ruined things, or had the time apart?

Disturbed at the thought, I started to babble.

"I've been dancing. Well, of course I have, but I got to dance the male lead in *The Nutcracker*. It's left me pretty exhausted, but there's no time to rest. We start rehearsals for the next production on Monday, and I can't help but hope I don't have a part in it. I mean, I have to have a part, but I hope I only have small ones. Counterproductive, right? I'm just so fucking exhausted; I don't want to take on the extra work. And the board of directors for my father's company has been hassling me to make an appearance. Oh, and remember Jon?"

Zeke looked like he was having trouble keeping up, but nodded and said, "The ginger," before turning the wipers on to brush away the now heavily falling snow.

"Right. Well, he kissed me on New Year's. I mean, I know people do that, but this was a real kiss. I didn't expect it at all."

Why the fuck was I telling him about it? Like I expected him to be jealous. Pathetic.

I fell silent, fingers fidgeting in my lap. Zeke looked like he'd tasted something bitter, and I wondered if he was annoyed at my sudden purge of words, or worse--thinking about what we'd done in the hotel room that night. I felt sick.

"I—I hope you don't...I mean, I'd hate for you to be, well, messed up by what happened between us," I said before I could stop myself.

Zeke frowned and glanced at me. "What does that have to do with anything?"

That hurt.

I remained silent the rest of the ride.

Zeke walked me up to my apartment, although I tried to talk him out of it. I'd decided the whole plan had been a colossally bad idea and just wanted to bury myself under the covers and try to forget.

My place was freezing. I nudged the thermostat so the heat kicked on and switched on a few lights while Zeke looked around.

"Wow. Pretty sparse."

"I haven't had time to decorate."

"How come you didn't stay in the dorms like you'd originally planned?"

He took off his coat, so I hung it next to mine in the closet, then circled the bar and put the kettle on to boil.

"It just didn't feel right anymore," I finally said. "I wanted to make a home, but I've kind of failed at that. Want some hot chocolate?" Why had he insisted on walking me up here, and why wasn't he leaving? Not that I wanted him to, but I'd certainly expected it, especially with the snow.

"Sure." Zeke sat down on the sofa, the only place to sit.

When I brought our cups, Zeke said, "Look, if you think you ruined my life that night, you can stop. I'm a big boy. I didn't do anything I didn't want to do. And I didn't text you back at Christmas because I thought it was better to just leave things as they were."

Yet he'd insisted on driving me home tonight. I cradled the red mug in my hands. "Okay. That's fair. And I'm glad you're okay — I know it's sometimes really hard for a guy to make that step."

Zeke shrugged, and I wished I knew what he was thinking. At least he wasn't protesting that he was straight and that night had just been a fluke. I kept talking because I couldn't not fill the silence.

"When I was sixteen, I slept with my best friend."

Zeke looked at me. "Nikki?"

I nodded. "I'd thought I wanted to. I mean, we were close, and she was pretty. I'd admired stuff about her, like what she wore and how she acted, and felt like I could spend all my time with her. I'd really thought I wanted her."

"And?"

I let out a breath. "It didn't turn out like I'd thought. She was visiting me in Milan, and we got a hotel room. After... uh... the sex, she asked me if I was gay."

Zeke's eyes widened, and he settled back into the couch. "Wow. That must have been a kick to the ego."

I chuckled, remembering how crestfallen I'd been. "Yeah, it was. I remember wondering why she'd asked. I mean, we'd both gotten off in the end, so I'd thought things had gone okay."

"Did you ask her why?"

"Yeah. She pulled the sheet down and asked me what I thought when I looked at her breasts. I said the first thing that came to my mind — that I wondered if it hurt when she ran."

Zeke laughed, and I smiled at the memory. "She looked at me and said, 'You don't want to slide your cock between them or anything like that?' I said, 'Well, I guess that would feel nice.' We ended up laughing, and later I'd had to admit to myself that maybe I liked guys more than I'd allowed myself to believe."

Zeke stared down at his hot chocolate. "When was your first time with a guy?"

I froze.

"Uh, I started experimenting after that. There were a few guys at the academy I fooled around with." Let Zeke think I'd slept with them. It was better than him knowing I'd given him my virgin ass like a love-sick boy.

Zeke looked into his cup. "I don't think I'm gay."

For once I tried to find the right words before I opened my mouth. "You could be bi."

Zeke scrunched up his face. "Is that really a thing?"

"Of course. Lots of people like both guys and girls. Isn't Dante bi?"

"Yeah. That's what he says, anyway." Zeke shrugged. "I dunno. I guess I thought saying you're bi was just a step toward admitting you're gay. You know, like saying you like guys but still like girls, too, and then eventually going completely with guys. Or the other way around, I guess, if you're a girl." He looked uncomfortable.

I shook my head. "People are definitely bisexual. I had several friends at the academy who were. It's a real thing. There are lots of sexualities, in fact, but I don't know enough to try to explain them to you."

Zeke seemed to be thinking about it. "So, I could really enjoy sleeping with both sexes."

"Of course. You don't have to pick one over the other to like better. Unless, you know, you want to. There aren't any set rules to a person's sexuality. It's an individual thing."

I watched Zeke's Adam's apple bob as he took a drink of hot chocolate.

"Also," I added, "some guys experiment, but it doesn't mean they want to be with another guy. Same with girls. Nikki said she once fooled around with her roommate at the dance academy, but she decided she wasn't into girls. She's never wanted to try it again."

Zeke's azure gaze fixed on me made my heart pound.

He set his cup on the table. "And if I wanted to try it again? What would that mean?"

I stilled. *Did he mean try again with me or with some other guy?* Imagining the latter twisted my stomach into knots, and imagining the former made my dick press against the front of my jeans. I lowered my cup to my lap.

"Um, I don't know? Nothing necessarily."

Before I could say anything else, Zeke leaned in and kissed me, tongue sliding into my mouth. Blindly, I managed to set down my cup before kissing him back.

Zeke murmured against my lips. "All I really know is I want to be inside you again."

I drew in a breath, tingling everywhere, and Zeke deepened the kiss, pushing me back into the cushions. I wrapped my legs around him. I couldn't believe he wanted me, but the stiff outline of his cock beneath his jeans proved that he did. I tugged on his hair and pushed up my hips, loving the deep groan that escaped from his mouth into mine.

"Fuck, Morgan," Zeke sighed into my neck moments later. We were both breathing hard. "Tell me you have a fucking bed."

I smiled into his hair. "Yeah. It's the only other piece of furniture I own."

We stood and made for the bedroom, shedding our clothes along the way between heated kisses that curled my toes.

On Sunday mornings, it had become a habit for me to veg out on the sofa and watch gay porn on my laptop. I'd learned a lot and had imagined doing so many things to Zeke's hot, hard, body. I'd never really thought I'd get the chance. I'd even looked up *Hard Time Productions* but got weirded out at seeing Hung on screen. They did mostly hetero porn anyway, and that did nothing for me.

Crawling between Zeke's muscular legs on the bed, I spent a long time tonguing his tight nipples, listening to his gasps turn to pants, and feeling his heart pound against my palm while his hands wandered over my bare skin. With a groan, he pulled me up and kissed me, hands kneading the cheeks of my ass like he owned it. When he touched my hole, I almost came.

"I want in there," he said, breaching me with his fingertip.

"I want you there." *God*, I kept expecting Zeke to back out. To realize he was wrong. But when I looked into his eyes, the desire I saw there incinerated me.

I moved away long enough to lean over and pull out the shoe box from under my bed. I handed Zeke a condom, and he ripped it open with his teeth, eyes never leaving mine.

"Roll it on me," he ordered. His flesh was warm and hard. I squirted lube on my fingers and reached back to prepare myself.

"Let me do that. Turn around."

Limbs shaking, I straddled Zeke's lap on my hands and knees, facing away from him. I watched myself reflected in the mirrored sliding closet doors across from my bed. My nipples were twin hard peaks on my flushed chest, my mouth was parted and my dark eyes wide. I looked drunk. Wanton. Behind me, Zeke concentrated intensely on what he was doing. When he brushed my hole with a wet thumb, I couldn't hold back my cry of pleasure, and when he slipped his finger inside me, I called out his name. Between our bodies, the tip of his sheathed cock touched my stomach.

"Please, Zeke," I whined.

"What?" He began moving his finger in and out of me, and I sobbed, it felt so good. Lowering my face to Zeke's bare legs, I licked and nibbled at his calves, loving the feel of the coarse blond hair against my face. I jerked when his finger ran over my prostate, and he did it again. And again. Until I was a writhing mess, my balls two tight orbs against my groin, and my shaft dripping and eager.

I was so damn close... teetering on the edge. When Zeke wrapped his free hand around my cock and tugged, I made an embarrassing sound halfway between a whine and a shout and spurted ropes of cum onto Zeke's thighs. Then I let out a yelp when Zeke leaned in and *bit my ass cheek*. Fuck, I'd never even imagined someone doing something like that.

Quickly, Zeke pulled me back, positioning me over his dick. I watched in the mirror as I sank onto it. The initial pain of entry was well worth the blooming pleasure. My chest rose and fell in quick pants as Zeke planted his feet on the bed and fucked up into me, powerful thighs tensing and balls bouncing with every thrust. I leaned backward and placed my hands on each side of him, a loud keen coming from my throat.

My dick flopped lewdly against my thighs with every thrust of Zeke's cock. I'd left the blinds raised that morning because the light on the ceiling had burned out. Outside my bedroom window, the snow continued to fall, laying a silent, heavy blanket over the world and casting an ethereal glow over the bed. The apartment had heated up quickly, and sweat ran down my body in rivulets. Sounds of slapping flesh and harsh breathing filled the room. In the mirror, my lean body arched backward over Zeke's muscular form. The sight of his cock moving in and out of my ass combined with the constant onslaught to my prostate had my dick filling again. A subtle tingling ran from my groin to my head, and I clenched around Zeke, a buzz setting up in my pelvic region. I suddenly felt like I had to pee, but the sensation faded as pleasure so intense I momentarily forgot where I was wrapped me in a warm cocoon before snapping apart like a stretched rubber band and sending me into free fall.

Through the waves of bliss, I felt Zeke's body stiffen, and my highly sensitized nerves picked up several things at once: Zeke's dick pulsing inside the thin layer of latex, his fingers digging into my sides, harsh, warm breaths hitting the back of my neck, and his body shaking between my knees.

When Zeke groaned and flopped back against the pillows, I eased off him and took care of the condom, body quaking through aftershocks. I grabbed some tissue from the box by the bed and cleaned us up.

"That was really something," Zeke said, eyes heavy-lidded and sexy as hell.

"Yeah." I sighed contentedly as I covered us with the sheet. My body still buzzed from the second orgasm, which had been more intense than the first, centering in the entire lower half of my body rather than just my dick and balls.

Looking out at the snow, I said, "I don't think you should drive in this. Stay here. They'll have it plowed by morning."

"Wasn't planning on leaving." Zeke tightened his grip around me and yawned before relaxing again. Moments later, he began to snore.

I lay awake for a long time, thinking. This probably didn't mean anything. I had to keep my head.

Eyes heavy, I eventually gave in to sleep.

CHAPTER ELEVEN

Zeke

I didn't know what it was about Morgan, but every time I was around the kid, my body lit up like a match to dry wood. And yeah, he didn't like it when I called him a kid, but he was only nineteen. I had eight fucking years on him. Eight years of hard living that someone like Morgan couldn't begin to imagine. Yet, he'd been the one explaining sexuality to me the night before, and sometimes I thought he'd learned more important things in his nineteen years than I had in my twenty-seven.

Labeling myself as bisexual was surprisingly freeing, as though sorting myself into a group proved I wasn't alone in this. Lying beside Morgan, his leg draped over mine, my father's and brother's voices in my head calling me a faggot and a pansy held less sting. It was like I didn't care so much anymore because I felt so damn good. What did it matter what my pop and brothers would say if they were here? They weren't here, and, although I'd tried to stop myself, the fact was I wanted to be with Morgan.

Unknown to anyone but myself, I'd gone to two performances of *The Nutcracker*, sitting stiffly in the audience dressed in a suit I'd borrowed from a friend. The first time, because I'd arrived late and hadn't yet looked at the program, I hadn't realized Morgan was behind the mask of the Nutcracker until he'd taken it off and become the prince, wearing a glittering gold jacket and soft boots and not a hell of a lot else. Not for the first time, I'd thought, *no wonder they call them tights*. My eyes had been riveted to Morgan's muscular ass for several long moments before I'd been able to lean back and enjoy the performance.

I'd known from watching rehearsals that those graceful moves were not as simple as they appeared for any of the dancers onstage. Even when Morgan was simply lifting the ballerina, he had to exert a lot of strength and poise to make it appear so effortless. I'd found myself annoyed by the expression of adoration on his face when he'd looked at the girl, even though I'd known it was all an act. Morgan was gay and definitely not in love with the chick playing Clara. In fact, I knew she was married to the guy who originally played the prince.

Before becoming Morgan's bodyguard, I'd thought all male dancers were gay. The fact some straight guys danced ballet had boggled my mind. But after watching day after day, I'd sort of been able to see what the allure was. I mean, these men were constantly surrounded by beautiful, fit women, and they did things with their bodies that had to feel as rewarding as any sport. Ballet certainly gave them terrific physiques. When I'd mentioned this to Morgan, he'd pointed out that some footballs players had improved their games by learning the basics of ballet. He'd also looked at me like he was proud of me for being so open-minded, and that had made me feel better than I ever would have imagined.

When Morgan as the prince had begun leaping around the stage, I'd held my breath in awe. He'd really looked the part of a young girl's—and I supposed boy's—fantasy, his face as gorgeous as his body and every movement perfect in its fluidity and grace.

The second performance had left me even more enthralled and knocked out by Morgan's talent than the first, and for weeks afterward, I'd beaten off to the memory of him in motion, along with those of the night we'd spent together in the hotel. I'd never believed I'd see him again face-to-face, which was why his appearance at the clubhouse had been such a shock. I'd been happy the heavy snowfall had given me an excuse to give Morgan a ride home.

When I'd seen the one-bedroom apartment with its blank white walls and sparse furniture, my heart had hurt for him. The place spoke nothing of the vibrant boy I knew. Morgan was too young to be living such a sterile, solitary life. I knew he could afford better; I hadn't missed the cashmere coat and leather gloves he'd worn the night before. The fact his folks' had sent him to school in Europe and had owned a company with a board of directors spoke of their wealth, and I'd always known Jake came from money, although he'd left all that behind. Morgan had both dough and class, and I had neither.

Morgan slept on his side, body half-covering mine. His hair smelled of floral shampoo. I ran my thumb up and down the length of his bare back, enjoying being close to him. The sheet lay bunched at our feet, or exertions having made us hot.

Eventually, I had to get up to take a piss. As with the rest of the apartment, the bathroom walls were stark white. The only splash of color came from a single blue towel hanging crookedly on the pewter rack above the toilet. A clear liner served as a shower curtain. There wasn't even a light fixture over the bare bulbs above the sink. Most hotel bathrooms I'd been in had looked more welcoming.

I studied myself in the mirror. The defeated look my face had held in the past weeks had been replaced by a sparkle in my eyes and upward curve to my lips.

Because of Morgan.

The kid brought light to my life that I couldn't deny but at the same time didn't know what to do with. I'd been scared. I'd wanted to reply to his text at Christmas, but I'd been too chicken-shit to do it, afraid of what might happen — or not happen — because of it.

Back in the small bedroom, I took a minute to enjoy the sleek lines and shadows of Morgan's body. The swell of his ass was even more beautiful bare than encased in tights, and remembering fucking it got me hard again.

God, he'd gripped me so damned tight — tighter than anything I ever could've imagined before our night in the hotel. Hell, I'd spent years trying to prove I was a real man thanks to my father and brothers, but, surprisingly, being with Morgan didn't make me feel like less of one.

I climbed into bed. Gently, I pushed back the lock of dark hair that had fallen over Morgan's smooth forehead before tracing his parted lips with my index finger. If he'd been awake, I would've nibbled at those plump lips and then rolled on top of him. Pushed his legs back and slid inside that narrow channel until my nuts pressed against his ass. What would it be like to fuck Morgan without a condom? My dick throbbed against my belly.

"What are you thinking about?"

Startled, I met Morgan's dark gaze. A feral smile stretched my lips. "Fucking you again."

Morgan chuckled. "My ass is still sore from the last time." He rolled over and looked at the clock. "An hour ago."

My smile dropped from my face. "Was I too rough?"

"No. You got me ready beforehand. But you are kind of big." His lips curled deliciously.

My chest might have puffed out a little. "Eight and a half inches."

"You measured?"

"Doesn't every guy measure his dick?" I lightly pinched Morgan's chest. "Come on. Admit it. You've done it."

"No, I haven't."

I reached between us and wrapped my fingers around Morgan's cock, pleased when it swelled against my palm. I stroked it.

"It's got to be a good six inches," I said. "You're a grower, while I'm a shower."

"Huh?" Morgan looked like he was trying to concentrate but couldn't quite do it. The little gasps he was making were hot as hell.

"You know. Your cock grows to its full length when you get hard. Mine is always the same size; it just gets stiff."

"Mmhmph..." Morgan's eyes rolled back in his head, and he arched his back, pushing his cock into my grip. My gaze wandered from the brown nipples on his toned chest down to his flat belly and the stark V leading to the trimmed patch of hair at the base of his cock. He had nice, round balls, and I suddenly remembered Morgan sucking on mine in the hotel. I wondered what it would be like to feel the weight of him on my tongue. Unease rippled through me. To fuck a man's ass was one thing, but to suck his cock?

Faggot.

"What's wrong?" Morgan asked, voice quiet in the semi-darkness, and I realized I'd stopped stroking him.

I swallowed. "Nothing."

The falling snow outside acted as a night light, illuminating the room just enough for us to see each other clearly. I started to stroke Morgan again, but he gently clasped my hand, entwining our fingers.

"Don't lie to me, please."

I met his gaze. "This is just different for me, that's all."

Morgan watched me intently. He didn't move or change expression, and gradually, I began to relax into the pillows.

"It's late," Morgan said. "No more thinking, okay? Let's sleep."

He closed his eyes, but I kept mine open, studying the lines of his face. The sharp cheekbones and dark eyebrows; the sweet, plump lips. I couldn't help it—I leaned forward and kissed him softly before settling down again. He smiled but didn't open his eyes. Before long, I drifted off and didn't wake until the glare from the snow outside filled the room with an intense brightness.

The space beside me was empty and cold. A note sat propped on the cardboard box Morgan had been using as a nightstand.

Roads clear. Went to rehearsal. Help yourself to coffee, but sorry there's not much food. Call me about the car. — M.

What had I expected, to wake up with Morgan's warm limbs still wrapped around me? Or maybe his mouth on my cock? I swallowed and sank back, taking myself in hand and thinking of everything we'd done the night before as I pleasured myself. I spread my legs and watched in the mirrored closet doors, imagining Morgan sitting on my dick as he had the night before as I quickened my movements and brought myself off in record time. I lay there, breathing hard for several moments before summoning the energy to clean up and make the bed.

I warmed the coffee that was in the pot in the microwave and drank a couple cups. He'd left a key to his place and a note on the bar asking me to lock up when I left. I fingered the key, wondering what it meant that he'd given it to me. Eventually, I had no more reason to stay and left the apartment, locking the door behind me.

Driving back to the clubhouse, I asked myself what it was I wanted.

I want him, came the immediate answer. I didn't know what that meant or how it would go, or even if Morgan wanted it, too, but I knew that I wanted to continue seeing him.

The clubhouse was buzzing with activity when I walked in. Everyone had returned from the rally and was getting ready for a big shoot. The dining room table was littered with coffee cups and donuts. I greeted them and headed straight for the shower. When I returned, the place was empty except for Dante and Swish, who sat at the kitchen table.

"Hey." I poured myself some orange juice.

"Hey." Swish yawned.

"How'd you enjoy riding bitch with the road captain?" I asked, and noticed Dante scowled a little. I wondered what was up there.

"I had fun," Swish said. "Ax is a good driver. Dante told me Morgan came by last night. Sorry I missed him."

"Where have you been?" Dante asked.

"I drove Morgan home. Roads got bad, so I stayed."

Swish made a noise of approval, and I looked over my shoulder to see Dante pulling a twenty out of a wad of bills and passing it to him.

"What the hell?"

Dante stuffed the bills back in his pocket and wiped his nose on some tissue. "Swish bet me you'd sleep with Morgan,"

My back to them, I struggled to keep calm and pulled out some bread to make toast. "Who said anything about sleeping with him?"

Swish lit up a cigarette. "You'd have to be dead not to feel the sex vibes between you two."

"I just thought it was mutual dislike, at least at first. Didn't know you were into guys," Dante said.

I glanced his way as I plucked the butter from the door of the refrigerator, feeling like I was edging toward a cliff.

"Neither did I," I said, jumping off. Either I'd hit the water and swim or dash out my brains on the rocks, but I wasn't going to hide what I felt about Morgan.

"So, you and Morgan are together?" Swish asked. He looked delighted.

"I don't know. Maybe. You and Morgan talk. Haven't you asked him?"

"Of course, but he always changes the subject."

I cleared my throat and concentrated on making my toast. "I don't know what we are."

When I sat at the table, Swish nudged the jelly in my direction.

"I think I might want us to be," I admitted. "Together." I looked up to catch Swish and Dante exchanging surprised looks. Apparently, they hadn't expected any real candor from me. Or maybe they'd thought I'd fuck Morgan and run.

"Morgan's great," Dante said. "You should go for it."

"He's pretty out of my league, and he doesn't have a hell of a lot of free time," I said. "He was up and gone before I woke this morning."

Swish smiled slyly. "As in, in his bed?"

I felt my face heating.

"Leave him alone," Dante said. "It's not easy figuring out you want something you didn't know you wanted."

I looked at him. "When did you figure out you were bi?"

"At a party for high school graduation. I was playing a drinking version of spin-the-bottle and the bottle landed on a guy. I'd always admired him but hadn't realized it was anything more than that. I thought he'd refuse to kiss and spin again, but instead, he leaned in and kissed me. What I felt when he did was difficult for me to reconcile in my mind."

I knew little about Dante's backstory, just that he came from a rich family. I had no idea what had brought him to the club. He was older than I was by a few years and had already been here when Blaze brought me in. For the first time, I wondered why I'd never bothered to ask him. As much as I considered the club my family, I sure didn't know much about them as individuals.

Swish looked mesmerized. "Did you get with the guy?" he asked. I'd never figured out what exactly was between Swish and Dante, but the air between them now seemed charged.

Dante shook his head. "No. I avoided the issue for a long time." The look on his face said he didn't want to continue with the conversation, so we dropped it.

I headed out to the garage. I was anxious to finish so I could get to the BMW and have an excuse to call Morgan. How pathetic was that?

The garage was cold, but I soon became overheated and pulled off my sweatshirt. My phone buzzed, and I slid out from underneath the Toyota to read the name on the screen.

"Hey, Scott, what's up?" I asked, wiping my greasy hands on a rag while balancing the phone on my shoulder. "I've been meaning to get with you to give back your suit."

"No rush. Just wanted to give you a heads up. Some dude's been looking for you. Older guy."

I froze.

"Who?"

"Dunno. Just that a guy's been asking around. Thought you might wanna know. Kinda resembled you. Your old man still alive?"

My stomach plummeted. "Uh, yeah. Could've been him."

"Okay. Wanna get together for a brew Friday night?"

"Maybe. Let me get back to you on that."

I disconnected and sat staring at the far wall. I hadn't been in touch with my pop or my brother Pete since Steve's funeral. I couldn't imagine what either of them would want with me now. I thought things were done as far as we were concerned, although, thinking back, Pop had acted like he'd wanted to talk to me at the service. I'd bolted out of there before he could get close.

But to want to talk to me enough to come looking for me?

Don't worry about it, I told myself as I slid underneath the car again. You're a grown man now. Even if your father were to walk through the door right now, there's nothing he could do to you.

Maybe it was time to let a little happiness into my life. I started whistling a tune as I picked up the torque wrench.

CHAPTER TWELVE

Morgan

"Try it again." Erik's voice echoed in the almost empty theater where he'd kept me behind to practice the fucking move that had been tormenting me for the past two hours. I was beginning to hate that fucking voice.

I didn't normally have trouble with the *pas de papillon*, also known as *jeté passé en arrière*, but that day I just couldn't seem to coordinate reaching the height needed in the first count with reaching the floor in the second count. I was frustrated and irritable, and it didn't help I hadn't heard from Zeke in more than a week. How long did it take to fix a fucking car, and didn't our night together warrant at least a text or two?

"Try it with your legs in low attitude until you can perfect the arm coordination," Erik suggested.

I stood bare-chested and dripping sweat, exhausted, but aware Erik wasn't going to release me until I got it right. I did as he said, concentrating more on my arms than my legs.

"Good, now try it properly," Erik directed after several attempts. He hit the remote for the music, and I stood in the pose *croisé derrière*, my right foot back *pointe tendue*. Taking a deep breath and blanking my mind so all I could hear and feel was the music, I stepped on my right foot in *demi-pliè in effacè en avant* while raising my left leg in back. I then sprang upward from my right foot and threw my right leg backward into the air while bending back my torso. Unlike past attempts, the movement felt smooth as my legs passed each other in the air, and when I landed on my left foot in attitude *croisé derrière*, exhilaration ran through me because I knew I'd gotten it right.

"Bravo." Erik looked pleased. He should be, as I was sure he was as eager as I was to get home.

"Once again."

I sighed and got back into position.

By the time I exited the building, it was well past midnight and every muscle in my body burned. I waved to Erik, and we went our separate ways. He'd asked me if I needed a ride, but the night was clear, and it was a relatively short walk to my apartment building. Besides, I knew he lived in the opposite direction. I'd pulled a pair of sweatpants over my leotard and tights and stuffed my feet into a pair of boots. The puffy jacket that I wore when walking kept me relatively warm in the January cold.

Every piece of me was tired, and my mind continued to go over the dance steps as though unaware that practice was over. My bag on my shoulder, I cut across the parking lot of the Arts Center toward the relatively empty road, breath smoky above the coil of plaid scarf wrapped around my neck.

When a car slowed on the street, I tensed. Occasionally, someone would catcall or yell something at me, especially if I was in tights, but I wasn't in this case and couldn't figure out why anyone would be pulling up beside me. That and the lack of lights on this particular street had me nervous. As the car crawled along, I looked straight ahead and waited for the driver to roll down his window and ask directions, but it didn't happen.

I glanced over. The car had tinted windows. *What the hell?* I began walking faster, and the driver accelerated to keep up with me. As soon as I could, I cut sideways behind a building, slipping through an alley between a restaurant and a dry cleaners and popping out on the other side, heart hammering in my chest. I made my way behind the row of stores in the general direction of my apartment building, although I was going to miss the mark by about a block when I came out on the other side.

When I found another opening, I circled back to the main street only to glimpse the car idling outside my building.

Who the hell was it, and how did they know where I lived?

Icy fear raced up my back as I leaned against the cold brick in the alley. What should I do? Walk boldly toward my building? Whoever was in the car could easily snatch me off the sidewalk, and as deserted as it was at that hour, any yelling I did wouldn't do me any good. If they wanted to take me, they could easily have done it while I was walking; that is, if there was more than one person in the car. Could it be someone who wanted to talk to me? Who? The Steel Pistons were the first to pop into my head, but Blaze had assured me they'd leave me alone. Could something have happened to negate the threat the Hedonists held over them?

I peeked again. The ominous car still sat in front of my building, exhaust rising in the cold air behind the rear bumper. I dug my cell phone out of my bag and scrolled through my contacts. Should I call the police? As scared as I was, I was still a little embarrassed to call and say I was hiding in an alley afraid to go into my building because of a car parked outside it.

Nikki would be asleep, and I wasn't sure having a tiny woman by my side would be much of a deterrent if this person wanted to hurt me anyway. Besides, I didn't want to put Nikki in danger.

I could call Jon or one of the other dancers, but knowing they were as exhausted as I was and had probably just dropped off to sleep made me hesitate. Erik had a wife and newborn baby at home. This wasn't necessarily an emergency. I would feel a fool if this was all a misunderstanding somehow and the driver of the car was waiting for someone in my building.

At 1 A.M.? I asked myself. Still, this was the city that never slept.

Zeke. Call Zeke. Being a general night owl, he would probably still be awake, and even if he wasn't, he didn't have a 6 A.M. job to get to. I'd feel safe walking into my building with Zeke, and it would give me an excuse to talk to him again.

Before I could argue myself out of it, I hit the call button while looking around the corner again to make sure the car was still there.

"'Lo?" Zeke's sleepy voice answered.

Seconds went by while I tried to think of what to say.

Shuffling at the other end of the phone. "Morgan?"

I let out a breath. "Yeah, it's me."

More rustling, as though Zeke was rolling over or sitting up.

"Is something the matter? It's late."

"Uh, well, sort of. I'm sorry. I didn't know who else to call."

"What is it?"

"I — well, it's probably nothing. It's just I was walking home, and this car started following me really slowly, and I veered off behind some buildings for a while, and when I came out...it's parked outside the front of my place. I'm afraid to go in."

"You got no idea who it is?"

"No. Do you think something happened and the Pistons are after me again?"

"I think if the Pistons wanted you, they would've already grabbed you off the street. What's the car look like?"

"Dark color. Um, I don't know, it looks similar to the club's SUV. Different model. It's just sitting there with the engine on. Fuck, maybe I should just walk in while talking to you."

On Zeke's end, I heard a door shut and a moment later an engine roar to life.

"Stay where you are; I'll be right there. I'm on my bike, or else I wouldn't hang up."

I stood shivering in the alley, hands pushed deep in the pockets of my puffy jacket, peering around the corner at the car, afraid if I took my eyes off it, I'd suddenly find myself face-to-face with some creep.

The car remained where it was. No one got out of it. With the tinted windows, it took an identity of its own, like it drove itself or something, which was creepy as hell to think about. I remembered some sci-fi story I'd once read that had something like that in it.

This late at night, Zeke could probably make the fifteen- minute drive in ten, but time seemed to stretch out to infinity. I was freezing. The buildings on each side of me afforded some respite from the bitter wind, but between where my coat ended and my boots began, my knees felt like ice cubes, the soft cotton of the sweatpants not enough to keep them warm when standing still.

It seemed obvious now the car wasn't waiting for someone. Who was driving, and what did they want from me? Where was Zeke? I looked at the time on my phone. He should have been there by now. My nerves jangled. I wanted to be inside. Safe.

Gripping my keys in my right hand so that one protruded between my fingers like a weapon, I counted to five and walked briskly toward my building, keeping my eyes straight ahead. When I got close, the motor of the idling car revved up as though about to begin a race, and I jumped at the unexpected sound before taking off at a run. I cleared the door of my building but didn't stop until I'd run up the two flights and down the hall to my door, hand shaking as I unlocked it. If the intention of the person in the car outside was to scare me, he was probably patting himself on the back about now. Unless...

Renewed fear seized me. I looked over my shoulder and breathed a sigh of relief to find the hallway empty. I skittered into my apartment, slammed the door, and locked it, securing the chain for good measure.

My living room window faced the front of the building, and I looked out in time to see Zeke hop off his motorcycle and approach the car that had been following me. As soon as he did, the driver pulled out of the space, almost knocking Zeke to the pavement, and sped off. Zeke looked left, then right and headed for the alley I'd been hiding in moments before.

I fumbled for my cell phone and dialed his number.

"Where the fuck are you?"

"My apartment. I made a run for it."

Zeke cursed and disconnected. I watched him retrace his steps and disappear under the awning of my building. Within seconds, he was pounding on my door.

I looked out the peephole before opening it and relocked everything once Zeke had stepped inside.

His expression was thunderous. "What was the point of calling me if you were just gonna take off on your own?"

"You were taking a long time, and I was freezing. I'm sorry I got you out here."

"There was a wreck on the parkway. God dammit, Morgan, that guy could have grabbed you!"

"So, it was a man?"

"I don't fucking know; the windows were tinted. I'm just assuming."

Still freaked out, I started pacing. "Maybe it was a stalker. Like, someone who watched me dance."

"Did they get out of the car when you walked by?"

"You mean ran by, and no, just revved their engine."

"Sounds like they wanted to scare you."

"They got their wish. But why?"

Zeke rubbed his eyes. "Who knows?"

"You really don't think it was the Pistons? I mean, I'm sure they're angry, so maybe they're just blowing off some steam."

"Maybe, although Blaze made it pretty clear they weren't to get within twenty feet of you, or we'd give the information to the Hogs. I don't think they'd want to risk what the Hogs would do to them just to blow off steam."

I took his coat and hung it next to mine in the closet by the front door. "Sorry I made you come all the way out here. Do you...just want to stay? It's after two."

When I turned around, Zeke's eyes held so much desire, my knees went weak. He strode toward me and lifted me up. I grinned as I wrapped my legs around his waist.

"What are you doing?"

Zeke carried me into my bedroom and deposited me on the bed.

"What does it look like I'm doing? I'm staying the night," he said and began to strip.

CHAPTER THIRTEEN
Zeke

Once again, like a love-sick fool, I lay with my head on my arm, staring at Morgan's sleeping face. Relaxed in sleep, he looked like something carved out of lightly burnished wood. I wondered if he had Greek ancestry. No matter how much I looked at him, I couldn't get enough, and that reality scared me less and less the more I was with him.

The night before, I'd met Scott at a local bar. The whole time, I'd expected my father to appear, but it hadn't happened. Why was he looking for me?

Thinking about the disgust he'd have on his face if he could see me lying in bed next to another man made me squirm, and I hated it. He had nothing to do with my life anymore, but imagining the things he'd say if he'd known I'd just had another man's dick in my mouth made my guts roil.

And whether I wanted to admit it or not, just the mention of him was having an effect on my life. Hell, when I'd left Morgan's place a week ago, I hadn't meant us to go so long without contact.

Fuck my father and his homophobic shit.

I hadn't been able to stop myself from tasting Morgan. The kid had been all jittery from being followed home, and all I'd wanted was to make him forget. I didn't think about the fact I was sucking on a man's cock, just that I was tasting Morgan, giving him pleasure. The sounds he'd made had challenged me to do even better, and soon a fog of lust had settled over me, blocking everything out but the two of us. I'd completely disconnected with the part of my mind that held my father's condemnations. When Morgan had come, he'd clutched my hair with both hands and bucked into the back of my throat, so deep I'd barely tasted his spunk. I had to admit I'd been a little disappointed about that, which surprised me even more than the realization I hadn't disliked him using my mouth like that.

The fear in Morgan's voice earlier that night when he'd called me had scared the shit out of me.

If I could've gotten close enough to the Dodge Durango with the tinted windows, I would have jerked the driver out of his seat and slammed him onto the pavement. As it was, the bastard had almost run me over. Who could it have been? I knew for a fact the Pistons didn't own an SUV, and even if they'd borrowed one, sitting and staring wasn't their style. Besides, no way were they going to take the risk of us sending their club to prison with the information we had on them.

So, who would be trying to scare Morgan? Thinking about it had me bristling. I wanted to rip out somebody's throat.

Morgan murmured and rolled over in his sleep, turning the smooth, olive-skinned expanse of his back to me. He was perfection, and I never stopped wanting to touch him. Hours earlier, I'd sat on the bed propped on pillows with Morgan straddling me. The sight of his body undulating as he'd ridden me, long-fingered hands against my tattooed chest, had amped up my desire for him, as had the noises he'd made when I'd run my tongue piercing over his flat, brown nipple and thrust my Prince Albert over his prostate. He made me feel powerful in a way I never would have imagined another man could. With Morgan, I felt whole and alive. Wanted.

Even more than that, the eye contact we'd shared while connected had moved me more than I could have ever thought possible.

I drifted off to sleep with the memory in my mind, and when I woke, disappointment washed over me at the cold, empty place beside me. Again.

"Good morning."

I couldn't control the smile that took over my face when I looked up to see Morgan approaching the bed with two cups of steaming coffee.

"Sit up. I got these a little too full."

I propped myself on the pillows and accepted the white cup with Dancers Do it with Attitude printed in bold black letters on the front. Morgan slid onto the bed beside me, carefully balancing his cup until he drained a good fourth of it.

"Want to go somewhere with me today?" I asked on impulse. "I mean, it's Sunday. You don't have rehearsals, right?"

The smile that lit Morgan's face made me forget my embarrassment at sounding so infatuated.

"Sure. Where do you want to go?"

I thought about it. "How about ice skating?"

Morgan looked inexplicably pleased by the suggestion. Then his brows went up. "You ice skate?"

"Why does that surprise you? I used to go most weekends growing up."

"I had you pinned as more of a skateboarder."

"I look like a skateboarder?"

Morgan laughed. "Is that an insult or something? I just thought you'd be too cool to ice skate, that's all."

"Ice skating's cool," I said. "Think of hockey players."

Morgan shook his head. "Of course. Forget I said anything. What do I know about being cool, anyway? I'd love to go."

We fell quiet, and I studied his face. It felt real domestic sitting there with him in bed drinking coffee.

"Something wrong?" I asked, because of the little frown line prominent between his dark eyebrows.

Morgan glanced at me, and for the millionth time, I was struck by how deep and dark his eyes were and how beautifully the lush lashes framed them.

"No. Just..." he bit his lip, and I waited. When I realized I was holding my breath, I let it out slowly and took another sip of coffee.

"I mean, is this a..." Morgan cleared his throat. "Is this a date?"

I barely managed not to choke. The uncertain look on Morgan's face made me rake up some courage.

"Yeah. It's a date."

The blush rising up Morgan's neck to suffuse his face was adorable.

"Okay." I could hear the smile in his voice behind his coffee cup. "Shower with me?"

I had no problem taking him up on that. Morgan on his knees, my cock stretching his mouth, started the day off with fireworks.

From that moment on, time fled. I couldn't believe it when the sun dipped behind the skyline. We'd skated for hours at Bryant Park Rink, joking around and talking like we'd known each other our whole lives. We'd raced, and I'd won, although his lithe body had given me a run for my money. Then we'd walked up to the Overlook and had hot chocolate while watching the skaters below.

Morgan had asked me more about myself, and I'd tried to share, although I'd skirted around my father's homophobia and the way I used to get beaten up when I'd hung around the house too long. Not for the first time, I wondered, *had my father sensed my bisexuality back then? Or had they all picked on me because I was quiet and scrawny?*

After Morgan finished relating one of Nikki's visits to Milan when they'd sneaked into the dance academy's kitchen and raided the pantry then had almost gotten caught by the sexy Italian administrator—and had spent the next hour or more fantasizing about what could have happened if the guy had caught them—I asked something I'd been wondering for a while.

"What's with the guilty look you get every time you talk about her?"

Morgan licked whipped cream off his upper lip and set his cup on the table. I wanted to kiss him so bad I couldn't stand it, but we were out in public, and I was nowhere near that brave. With a woman, it would have been so easy. For the first time, I considered how cheated gay men and women must feel.

"I look guilty?"

"Yeah. I noticed it right away. You drop her or something?"

Morgan frowned. "Huh?"

"Dancing, I mean. Did you cause the injury that made her have to quit?"

Morgan's face cleared. "No, no. I didn't realize I look guilty when I talk about her. I guess... I guess I feel guilty because Nikki and I have always had the same dream, and now I'm living it, and she can't."

"That's not your fault."

"I know. And don't think Nikki hasn't said the same thing to me plenty of times. I guess she's seen it on my face, too. I didn't realize I was so transparent."

I shook my head. "Just don't ever play poker."

A splatter of whipped cream landed on my face, and I wiped it off with a napkin before pinning Morgan with a look of intent. "You're gonna regret that when we get back to your place."

Morgan laughed. "Oh, what're you going to do, suck my brains out through my cock again? I'm so scared."

I refrained from looking around to make sure no one heard. He hadn't said it loud, and if he wasn't worried, I shouldn't be. I tilted my head and gave Morgan my best sexy look. Besides, I wanted to hear more about my blowjob skills. "That good, huh?"

"Well, not bad for a novice."

"Yeah? Well, my head still hurts from you yanking on my hair the whole time."

Morgan's face turned pink.

"You're cute when you blush."

"I'm not blushing."

"Yeah, you are."

I brushed my knee against his under the table, and the look he gave me was scorching hot.

"Maybe we ought to head back to my place now," he said huskily.

I was totally on board with that.

In the cab on the way, I kept my hand on Morgan's knee, fingers occasionally running along the inside seam of his jeans. I enjoyed teasing him, and the cab driver couldn't see what I was doing. Morgan's cell phone rang. He answered it, tensing as though he wasn't fond of who was on the other line. I listened to his monosyllabic replies, curiosity mounting, until the cab pulled to the curb in front of Morgan's building, and he disconnected.

"Who was that?" I asked after we'd paid the driver.

Morgan shoved his cell phone into the pocket of his coat. The tip of his nose was red from the cold, and I wanted to kiss it.

"Gerald Peters. Basically the thorn in my side."

Anger stirred in my chest that someone was bothering him. "Who the fuck is he?"

We entered the building and headed for the elevators only to find they were out of order. Morgan cursed, and we turned toward the stairs.

"This place is a dump," he muttered.

"You're preaching to the choir. Now, who is this Peters guy?"

114

"The president of my father's company. My company."

"What's he want?"

"Just to hassle me about stuff. He doesn't like me being CEO. I hold the majority of shares since my parents died. Actually, I get the feeling nobody on the board is very happy about that."

"What kind of company is it? Jake never talked about it."

"He wouldn't have. Jake wanted nothing to do with Wentworth Properties. We own a bunch of apartment complexes and vacation rentals. A few strip malls. Stuff like that."

The pieces clicked into place in my mind. "Wentworth Building belongs to your family?" I couldn't believe it. I knew the kid had money, but I didn't know he was fucking loaded. "Why the hell do you live here, then?"

"Hey, it's not so bad."

"You just called it a dump."

"I was aggravated because of the elevators. I like my apartment."

We turned the corner and climbed the second flight of stairs.

"Here we are busting our thighs 'cause the elevator's broken, when you can afford someone to carry us to your apartment on their backs," I teased.

Morgan laughed and shook his head. "I like doing things for myself."

"Why don't you live in the penthouse of your family's building? It's yours, isn't it?"

"I rent it to my COO—the guy who called just now. I wasn't going to kick him out when I got back from Milan. Besides, I don't need a big place like that."

When we reached Morgan's floor, somebody's dog started yipping like crazy behind a closed door. I followed Morgan down the hall and waited while he unlocked his.

"Yeah, this shoe box is much better than any big, luxurious penthouse," I muttered as we walked in.

Morgan elbowed me. I was still reeling from finding out he was a *Wentworth* Wentworth. His brother had shunned all that money, and Morgan preferred to live in a tiny, nondescript apartment rather than the penthouse of a luxury building that he fucking owned. Coming from a poor family, I just didn't get it.

"What was that Peters guy hassling you about?" I asked.

Morgan dropped his keys on the bar and turned to me.

"Last week, I attended a board meeting and got a nasty surprise."

I wondered how the fuck the kid had the time to attend a meeting with the dance schedule from hell but didn't interrupt.

"Jon's brother approached me about needing a place for an LGBTQ center he wants to start in the Bronx, and I thought of the perfect building. The board didn't agree with me. They don't want to do it."

"How come?" I asked.

"They didn't give me a good reason. It's not like we'll lose a lot of money—that building's sat vacant for years. It needs a lot of work, but Jon's brother has volunteers willing to fix it up." Morgan sighed. "When I'm at the board meetings, I feel like they're patronizing me, and I can't say much about it because I haven't been around. They don't take me seriously."

Anger on Morgan's behalf gathered inside me.

"You're a fucking Wentworth. You own the place. They damned well have to take you seriously. If you want an LGBTQ center in a building you fucking own, you get to have one."

Frustrated, I looked around the bare apartment. "And do you think you insisting on living in this place might have something to do with them not taking you seriously? Why the hell haven't you fixed it up? You only have two pieces of furniture, for Christ's sake."

Morgan sat on the couch and leaned into the cushions. "I don't have time for that. Besides, what's the point?"

Inexplicably eager to do something for the kid, I paced the floor. All I knew is I wanted to put a smile on his face, but more than that, I wanted him to believe in himself.

"The point is, if you want people to take you seriously, you gotta play the part. If you won't live in your penthouse, you gotta at least fix up the place you do live in. You're off today and have me to help you, so there's no excuse not to."

Morgan sank deeper into the couch. "It's late, and we just got home." It was almost a whine. As much as I called him "kid," I sometimes forgot he was only nineteen. And that only made me sadder that he lived the way he did.

"You got a laptop, don't you? This is 2018. Nothing says we can't order furniture at night while lying naked in bed. Come on."

The smile that lifted Morgan's lips was nothing short of naughty. "Now you're talking."

CHAPTER FOURTEEN

Morgan

Zeke came back three days later to oversee the furniture delivery. When I got home from rehearsal, I was worn out, but seeing everything already unboxed and put together rejuvenated me. As did the large three-meat pizza Zeke had ordered.

In just a few days, so much had changed. I had a comfortable place to come home to, and maybe a boyfriend. I still couldn't believe Zeke didn't have a problem being with a guy, but other than a vague unease when in public, that seemed to be the case.

My apprenticeship with Manhattan Ballet continued to leave me with nearly no time for anything else, but I'd always known it would be that way. What I hadn't known was there would be someone I'd want to spend time with, and that I'd take an interest in the family company. The day I'd gone to the board meeting, I'd sat down with a few heads of departments at Wentworth Properties and been surprised at the interest that had sparked within me. I had a good team there, some with great ideas for change. George Peters had been present, but he hadn't said much. I continued to get the feeling he didn't want me there and would prefer that I'd let the other shareholders buy me out.

Zeke came over most nights. Kissing him became my favorite pastime. When he covered me with his big body, I melted into him. He finished with the car, brought it back to me, helped me sell it, and I gave the money to the LGBTQ center.

Zeke helped me decorate my apartment. I couldn't have—hell, *wouldn't* have—done any of it without him. I found dance prints to cover the walls, an over-sized chair in my favorite shade of red with a comfortable ottoman to match, a big screen TV, and a bookshelf to fill with my favorite novels. I came home at night and wrapped myself like a burrito in a soft, gold throw and watched television, a scented candle burning on the mahogany coffee table in front of me. If Zeke was there, he curled up with me. After years of dorm living, the domesticity of it all clenched at my heart and often brought tears to my eyes.

And the weird thing was, I felt better with a nice-looking apartment. Maybe that translated to my taking myself more seriously. Zeke was right; I could have that LGBTQ center if that's what I wanted, and I was going to tell Peters that.

I didn't know what Zeke and I were to each other, or how long it was going to last; but the more time that passed, I did know that when it ended, it was going to wreck me. I couldn't realistically believe Zeke would want to stay with me forever. Not when he was just finding his sexuality, and not with the schedule I kept. But I pushed all that to the back of my mind, not wanting to ruin the time we did have together.

"Maybe it won't ever be over," Nikki said one night over salads from a nearby deli when I'd voiced my thoughts about it.

I snorted. "What, you think we'll get married one day? Not likely. I still can't believe we're doing what we're doing. I was so sure Zeke was one of those closet cases."

"He's good for you, right? I mean look at this place." Nikki gestured around the living room. "Why do you have to make problems for yourself?"

My eyes widened in disbelief. "Excuse me, but aren't those the words I should be saying to you? I ran into Paul when I was grocery shopping the other night. He said you never got in touch with him after that night outside your building."

I almost felt bad at how Nikki's face fell at my words. Almost. Somebody needed to knock some sense into her, and I was more than happy to get the spotlight off myself.

"Call him," I said, taking her cell phone off the table and tossing it into her lap.

"And say what?"

"That you miss him. That breaking up with him was a mistake because you're delusional and have weird ideas about your own happiness. That you'll do anything to get him back."

"That's going a little far, don't you think?"

"How badly do you want him?"

Nikki looked at the phone in her lap. "Pretty badly."

"Then it's not going too far."

"Okay, I'll call him, but not here. I'll need privacy. And maybe some liquid courage."

"Promise me."

Nikki rolled her eyes. "Okay, okay, I promise." She tossed her fork onto her plate on the coffee table. "Time to change the subject. What's going on with the LGBTQ center? Last you said, the board didn't like the idea of housing it in one of their buildings."

"Zeke says as the CEO, if I want it, I should have it."

"Sounds like good advice."

"He says I have to take myself seriously before anyone else will, which was part of the reason why he encouraged me to fix up this place."

Nikki nodded. "That is, if you're sure you want to run a multi-million-dollar company. You don't have to, you know. I really don't see how you have the time."

"All I know is I don't want to look back one day and regret giving it up."

Nikki regarded me a moment. "I'm proud of you, Morgs. And I believe in you. I just hope you don't drive yourself into the ground trying to be everything you think you should be. It's okay to admit you can't do it all or that you don't want to."

"I'll do my best. It's not like I want to completely take over anytime soon. I just want to have a hand in things. An LGBTQ center in that part of the city would be a great addition to the community. I don't know why the board is so against it, but in the end, it's my choice."

"Are they homophobic?" Nikki asked.

I scratched my head. "I don't know. It kind of points that way, doesn't it?"

"If they are, and they know or have guessed you're gay, it might be the reason they don't come out and say that's why they don't want the LGBTQ center in one of your buildings."

The idea that my father's board of directors didn't approve of the LGBTQ community made the food I'd eaten try to climb back up my throat. Was it just the board, or had it been my father as well? Allen Wentworth had known the people who sat on his board very well. Most were good friends, and all had been present at the company's genesis. Had my father been a homophobe? I'd never told my parents I was gay; there'd never been an opportunity. If they'd lived, would they have been ashamed of me?

Nikki began talking about work. After she'd broken up with Paul, she'd changed jobs, unable to face him every day. Now she was employed as a hostess at an upscale restaurant and had plenty of stories about people who came and went. She was planning a trip with her sister to Barcelona in a couple of months.

"I'll send lots of pictures and let you know," she said, and I realized I'd zoned out. I smiled and nodded and tried to focus. Another hour went by as we emptied a bottle of wine.

"Want to sleep here?" I asked her. "You can't drive tipsy."

Nikki nodded, so I went into my room to find her something to wear, returning with an old T-shirt of mine and a pair of boxer shorts. She'd made up the couch with a sheet, blanket, and pillow from the closet, and I told her goodnight.

Lying in bed, our earlier conversation resurfaced, keeping me from sleep. I looked at the time on my phone. Half past ten. I dialed Harvey's number.

"Sorry to call so late," I said when he answered.

"No problem, Morgan, I wasn't asleep. What can I do for you?"

I explained what was going on with the board and the LGBTQ center. "Got any idea why they'd be so against it? They haven't given me a concrete reason."

I'd hoped there was some other explanation for it, and my heart sank at Harvey's reply.

"I'm afraid I do have an idea," Harvey said. "Wentworth Properties has a slightly rocky past with the LGBTQ community. I'm afraid you've barely avoided a few discrimination lawsuits."

"What? How have I never heard about this?"

"It all happened while your father was in charge of the company. I know of at least two instances in the past where gay tenants were evicted from Wentworth buildings due to their sexual orientation."

"But... that's against the law!"

"The official reason for the evictions was noncompliance, but the fact is Wentworth Properties paid them off."

"So... my father was a bigot?"

"Not necessarily. At least, he's never voiced such feelings in front of me, and I knew him a long time. Wentworth Properties caters to large businesses, and some of them aren't as open-minded as they should be. My guess is your father had been trying to keep these customers happy. Morgan, Peters called me about your desire to create the center. He pointed out it would cause problems with Albert Easter."

"Of Easter Furniture?" Albert Easter was one of our biggest clients with stores all over the eastern United States. It irked me that Peters would tell this information to Harvey and not to me. Harvey had been sitting in for me, after all. I may have been absent before, but I was back now. It seemed Peters considered that Harvey, as my former guardian, acted as a father figure to me. That Peters tried to go over my head to my "daddy" infuriated me.

"As well as Spiffy Cleaners. What you might not know is Easter's father-in-law is Fred Starborn, the TV Evangelist who speaks publicly against homosexuality and the disintegration of the nuclear family. I hadn't known it. Peters says Starborn has a lot of hold over Easter. I'm sure you realize Wentworth Properties would take a major hit if they lost Albert Easter's business."

I set my jaw. "I'm not going to support discrimination, under any circumstances, and particularly not so close to home. And why the hell didn't Peters tell me all this himself?"

Harvey was silent a moment, then sighed.

"He doesn't realize you're capable, Morgan. You've got to show him. Prove him wrong."

It was my turn to be silent.

"Oh, and Morgan. I've been meaning to talk to you about drawing up a will. You need to name a beneficiary."

Not something else I need to do, I inwardly groaned. "Is that really necessary?"

"I'm afraid it is. If something were to happen to you, a judge in probate court would name an executor to handle your estate. Likely, in order to protect their interests in the company, the board would ask Gerald to continue to run Wentworth Properties until your estate is settled, which could take years. You can't leave something like that dangling. I know you're young, but with such a large estate, you need a will. Not having one would be the height of negligence."

I closed my eyes. "All right. I'll come in one day this week during my lunch."

"I'll have it all drawn up for you. You can give me a name then."

I thanked Harvey and hung up, aware there was only one person in the world I had that I could leave my estate to, and that was Nikki. While she would certainly be better than no one, she had no business sense and plenty of her own money.

What about Zeke? My mind supplied. As far as I could tell, he had nothing but the MC and the clothes on his back. But he and I hadn't known each other for long, and it seemed kind of crazy to leave my fortune to him; yet, he'd given me great advice so far.

It's not like you're likely to die anytime soon, I told myself. You just need a name for your will. You can always change it later. Besides, the part of me that insisted I cling to my company also told me Zeke was trustworthy.

I rolled over and sighed. If that voice was the angel on my shoulder, the devil on my other shoulder rose up to make me second-guess myself. I was nineteen-years-old and had no one, yet I was clinging to a company I'd never had an interest in before the death of my parents. I was the last of the Wentworths, and as a gay man, unlikely to sire an heir. Dancing had been my life as long as I could remember. As busy as I was, logic said the smart thing to do would be to let the other stockholders buy me out, right? How much easier would my life be if I did? No more worrying and spreading myself too thin. No more weight of family duty on my shoulders. I could concentrate on dance and only dance.

But, if I had to stop dancing for some reason, such as an injury, which happened a lot in ballet, I wouldn't have the company to fall back on. And when I imagined the large, imposing Wentworth building with someone else's name on it, I balked. Sure, if I sold the company, I could stipulate the name must remain, but I couldn't get past the fact that letting it go would be letting go of my legacy. Was I wrong to hope there could be something in me that might successfully run the place someday? At least as the main shareholder, I could keep it in the family until I could make that decision.

When my father was alive, I would have laughed at the thought, but now that he was gone, the idea didn't seem so funny anymore.

When Jon's brother had come to me about the LGBTQ center, he'd planted a seed. I wanted to do more than simply run Wentworth Properties; I wanted to use my name and money to make a difference. I *would* make a difference.

The phone rang, and I swiped it open, thinking Harvey had forgotten something and called me back. Who else would ring so late?

"Hello?"

Nothing on the other line.

"Hello?" I said again. After a moment of silence, I heard rustling on the other end. I looked at the screen, but it said unknown. I could hear someone breathing, and the noise grew louder after a few seconds. Annoyed, I disconnected, rolled over, and drifted off to sleep.

CHAPTER FIFTEEN
Zeke

"What exactly is going on between you and Morgan?" Blaze asked one evening after I'd come in from the garage. He sat at the kitchen table going over something for Hard Time Productions. I'd been working like a demon to fix the cars I had waiting, so I'd have some free time to spend with Morgan that Sunday.

I took a moment to think while I washed my hands at the kitchen sink. It wasn't like I thought Blaze would judge me, but it felt funny telling him I was involved with Jake's little brother.

"Zeke?"

I turned and looked at him. "We're kind of seeing each other."

"Kind of?"

"Okay, we are seeing each other."

"Oh." Blaze looked down at the papers in front of him. I couldn't read his expression.

"Does it bother you?" I asked, taking longer than necessary to dry my hands, nerves jangling at the thought of Jake's disapproval. The club was the only family I had.

Blaze licked his lips. "That depends."

My stomach cramped. "On?"

"What your intentions are, I guess." He chuckled. "I sound like a dad, don't I? But Jake was my best friend, and he isn't here anymore to look after Morgan. The kid hasn't got anybody. And as close as you and I are, I can't help but wonder what an older guy who I didn't even know swung that way wants with him. Unless..."

I straightened my spine, jaws clacking together. "You think I want Morgan for his money."

Blaze had the decency to look contrite. "I've never thought you cared much about money. Maybe I just wonder if he's an experiment for you. Just... help me understand, man."

I sat down at the table and lit a cigarette from the pack in front of Blaze. "When I understand, I'll be the first one to let you know."

I took a deep drag and let it out, meeting Blaze's eyes. "My attraction to Morgan was instant. Explosive. I was confused and channeled it into anger. Anger that you'd sent me to get him, that he was a dancer, that Jake had left it to us to take care of him." I shrugged. "Once I really got to know the kid, I liked him as a person, and then I couldn't get the physical attraction out of my head. Morgan's caring, funny, understanding. He doesn't judge me for being a mechanic with a GED. He makes me feel things I've never felt before. And he's..." I paused, wrapped up in my thoughts, "he's... beautiful," I finished quietly.

When I looked at Blaze again, he looked stunned.

"You're in love with him."

"What? No, I—"

"It's written all over your face."

I frowned. Instead of arguing about something I wasn't so sure wasn't the truth, I asked, "Did you know Morgan and Jake were *the* Wentworths? The ones with the fancy building uptown?"

"Yeah. Didn't you?"

"Hell, no. I knew Jake came from money, so of course Morgan had to, too. But I never connected the dots until recently."

"J wasn't one to talk about all that, but I knew it."

I shook my head, thinking of Jake and Spoons' girl. "You ever think letting Vanessa work at Hard Time was a mistake? Jake probably wouldn't have met her otherwise."

"We don't know that." Blaze sighed. "I've gone over it all so many times in my head, but what's done is done. The only thing I can control now is Morgan's safety. J never stopped worrying about all the responsibility Morgan was taking on. He felt bad that he'd skipped out and didn't shoulder some of it. He also thought his dad's friends at the company were douche bags."

"I don't think Morgan likes them much, either."

"When you going to see him again?" Blaze asked.

"Sunday, if I can get these cars finished in time." I got up from the table and fished around in the refrigerator until I found some baloney to slap between two pieces of bread.

"So," Blaze said slowly, "uh... not to get too personal, but how's the sex? I mean, with another guy. Must be different for you."

I leaned against the counter, took a bite of my sandwich and considered. It felt a little weird to talk about it, but then again, I was closer to Blaze than anyone in the club. I also sensed something underlying Blaze's curiosity.

"Yeah, different. But surprisingly good. I mean, I was shocked at how easy it was. I guess, if I'm honest with myself, I'd always found something attractive about... about guys."

"Really?" Blaze looked like he really wanted to know, so I tried to put my thoughts into words.

"When I was growing up, Pop always called any guy he didn't think was the ultimate example of manliness a fag or a queer. He and my brothers would get onto me, because I was small and scrawny back then. You remember how I looked. Now I wonder if they'd seen something in me. If they'd known, you know? I mean, I like women, but I guess I'm bisexual. Morgan says that's a real thing."

Blaze nodded. "Judging by the assortment of men and women coming and going from Dante's bedroom, it's definitely a real thing."

"How come you're asking me about this?" I asked.

Blaze looked away. "No reason. Just curious, I guess." He smiled, but I got the feeling it was sort of faked. "I think Morgan's a great guy, and I'm glad you're together. I'll worry about him less from here on out."

I washed down the rest of my sandwich with some orange juice. "How are you and Katie doing?"

"We broke up."

I set my glass in the sink and turned back to Blaze. "When?"

"A couple nights ago."

"How'd she take it?"

"What makes you think she didn't break up with me?"

"Because you never stay with a girl for long. I'm beginning to think you've got commitment issues, man."

"She took it pretty hard. Cried and then started throwing things at me."

"Shit."

"Yeah."

Something was off. Blaze seemed distracted. I didn't want to pry, though. He'd tell me if and when he wanted.

"Guess I'll get back to the cars," I said, and when Blaze didn't say anything else, I headed out to the garage.

I'd left my phone on the workbench and smiled when I saw a text from Morgan. He must be on his lunch break.

Morgan: *What are you wearing?*

Me: *A greasy shirt and a pair of jeans.*

Morgan: *Sounds sexy. Got your jacket on?*

I couldn't help but smile while typing out the answer.

Me: *No, Mom.*

Morgan: *You'll catch cold.*

Me: *Never do. What are you doing?*

Morgan: *On my way to my lawyer's office. Got to sign some papers.*

I wondered what kind of papers but didn't want to horn into his business.

Morgan: *See you Sunday?*

Me: *You got it. Take time for lunch.*

Morgan: *Yes, Mom.*

I doubled my efforts to get the work done.

CHAPTER SIXTEEN

Morgan

When I arrived at his office, Harvey had lunch ready for me. I was still smiling from texting with Zeke when I walked in; and, aware of my tight schedule, Harvey immediately sat me down to eat while explaining the legalese of the will.

"And your beneficiary?" Harvey asked.

"Zeke Ivers." I passed him a piece of paper with Zeke's contact information.

"Forgive me, Morgan. I only ask because we've known each other a long time, and I've been in the position of being responsible for you. Are you certain about this person? I've never heard you mention him before."

"Absolutely. He's a long-time friend of my brother's as well as a friend of mine."

"All right, then." Harvey had me sign several papers, and we spent the rest of the meal chatting.

"I hope you won't mind, but I have a favor to ask you," Harvey said as we were finishing up.

"Sure. Anything I can do for you, I will. You've been a good friend to my dad and to me."

Harvey smoothed down his thick salt and pepper hair and regarded me fondly. "I wondered if you would consider accompanying Janine and me when we escort a good friend and important client to an art gala tomorrow evening. He's visiting from out of the country, and we want to show him a good time. He loves art and follows the ballet. And, well, he's a big admirer of yours."

I hesitated. "A blind date? I'm kind of seeing someone."

Harvey shook his head. "No, just a fourth for the evening. Tomas attended a performance of *The Nutcracker* when he visited friends in the city over Christmas, and he recently mentioned he'd love to meet you."

"Really?" I couldn't help but be flattered, and it would please me to do something in return for all Harvey's past kindnesses as well as his continual support of my decisions. But, as always, there was my tedious schedule to consider. "I have rehearsal."

"The showing isn't until ten o'clock. We'll have a late dinner afterward. Perhaps Elias will let you out early just this once if I drop him an email? We're old friends."

I smiled. "If you can make it happen, I'm willing."

"Wonderful. I'll give you the address of the art showing, and you can meet us there after rehearsal."

"I may be a little late," I warned him.

"No problem. We'll see you there."

I left, hurrying down to the Uber Harvey had called for me. Glancing at my phone, I saw I was going to be about ten minutes late back to the theater, but with luck, I could slip in without anyone noticing.

As it happened, Erik definitely noticed, and I had to endure a twenty-minute lecture after practice about the importance of being punctual and how no apprentice was guaranteed a place in the company.

Properly chastised, I exited with my tail between my legs and headed home. In my apartment, I'd left the small lamp on next to the couch, and it cast a welcoming glow over the living room. I showered, ate some fruit and grilled chicken, and headed for bed, which seemed empty without Zeke there. Funny how I could get so used to having him next to me in such a short amount of time.

My phone buzzed in the darkness, and I reached for it, already smiling at the thought of a goodnight text from Zeke. Instead, I found a number with an area code I didn't recognize.

Morgan, this is Tomas Marchant. I hope you don't mind I asked Harvey for your number. I just wanted to say I'm looking forward to meeting you tomorrow night.

Harvey had insisted the evening wouldn't be a date, so what was with the text? I considered a moment before deciding not to text back. Exhausted and sore as I was from the grueling hour I'd spent with Erik making me go over the same routine again and again until he tired of me and went on to torture someone else, I popped some ibuprofen in my mouth and washed it down with water before settling into bed and falling to sleep easily.

C3&O

Located at the top of a building in Lower Manhattan that was coincidentally owned by Wentworth Properties, the gallery was packed to the gills with visitors holding plastic champagne flutes and meandering around the space examining the artwork. The press was there, shooting photos of the artists and various important guests. Ten-thirty wasn't considered late for New York City, but most hadn't spent the past twelve hours leaping around a stage and lifting one hundred and ten-pound women as I had. My hips ached and my feet were numb. I scanned the room for Harvey's salt and pepper hair and signature red tie but didn't see him.

One side of the large, modern, white-walled room had been reserved for the showcased artist, David Martel, whose work I had heard about but never seen up close. I was drawn to the series of sketches lined up across one wall. Martel's preferred medium was charcoal, and I admired the varying strokes, some bold, some thin, some barely there, and some deeply shaded—all coming together to form stark images of love, life, death, and creation.

"Beautiful, aren't they?" a deep, accented voice spoke near my ear.

"Very." I turned to find an impeccably dressed man at my side, tall and dark with sparkling hazel eyes and a Roman nose. He looked slightly familiar, and I realized I'd seen his photo in the society pages. He held out his hand, and I shook it.

"Tomas Marchant."

I raised my brows.

"Morgan Wentworth."

A grin softened the other man's features, forming a fan of lines around his eyes. He had to be well into his forties and was quite handsome.

"Believe me, I know. I am an enthusiastic patron of the arts." Marchant's voice was heavily accented.

"I'm flattered." I looked around. "Where are Harvey and Janine?"

131

"They slipped downstairs to see the metal reliefs and will be back up presently. Champagne?" Marchant gestured to a waiter making the rounds with a tray.

I shook my head.

"Are you certain? It's very good."

"I'm sure it is, but I'm afraid I'm not old enough to drink." I held up the water bottle I'd taken from the table in the front.

Rather than embarrassed, Marchant looked delighted. "It is easy to forget you are so young in the face of all you have accomplished. On your way to joining one of the most prestigious corps de ballet in the world, and Chief Director of a multi-million-dollar company. Quite impressive. Most of us work our whole lives for much less."

"I didn't exactly have to work to obtain my company," I said. "I more or less own it by default. And I certainly don't run it. Not yet, anyway."

Marchant smiled. "I appreciate your modesty as well as your spunk. So, if I should be interested in purchasing a few properties, you would not be the one for me to talk to?"

I felt myself coloring. Humility was one thing, but I hadn't meant to make myself out to sound ineffectual. "You can definitely talk to me."

He smiled. "Good. I will look forward to it."

I focused my attention on the sketches again while Marchant kept up a steady stream of commentary. By the time Harvey and Janine joined us, I'd become comfortable with the man.

"Morgan, you made it." Harvey patted me on the back, and I exchanged kisses and hugs with Janine. Not conventionally pretty, Janine's attractiveness came from her good-humor, sharp intellect, and uncanny ability to size up a situation at a glance. She hooked arms with me and led me away from Harvey and Tomas Marchant.

"He can be a bit too much," she whispered in my ear.

I laughed. "I guess so, but he's entertaining. I was unsure of what to expect after he texted me last night."

Janine stopped walking. "He did? I'm very surprised Harvey would give him your number."

"Marchant probably told him it was business. He's interested in some properties."

Janine nodded. "That must be it. Tonight isn't meant to be a fix-up, just a comfortable evening among friends. Tomas admires you, and as an important client, Harvey wants to keep him happy."

I nodded. "He hasn't indicated otherwise."

By the time we left the art gallery, my stomach was growling enough for the others to hear it.

Harvey smiled at me in the rearview mirror of his silver Volvo where I sat in the backseat with Janine, who had insisted Marchant sit in the front passenger seat next to Harvey, evidently protecting me.

"Don't worry, I've ordered ahead at a small Cuban restaurant owned by a friend. We'll be there shortly," Harvey said. "I'm sure you're famished, Morgan, after dancing all day."

I smiled and nodded, adjusting my blue silk tie and listening to Janine talk about the book she'd recently finished reading. Something on the New York Times bestsellers list, but I'd missed the title. Reading was just one more thing on the long list of things I wished I had time to do.

My phone buzzed in my pocket, and I took it out.

Zeke: *Rough day?*

Me: *Very.*

Zeke: *Want some company?*

Surprised, my thumbs hovered over the screen.

Me: *I thought you were working?*

Zeke: *I am, but I could use a break. I can leave in the morning when you do and get back at it.*

Me: *I wish I'd known. I'm out with friends.*

It took a while for Zeke to text me back, during which time Marchant peppered me with questions about Milan. When my cell phone finally buzzed, it took everything I had not to rudely dismiss the man to read the text. Finally, Harvey snagged his friend's attention, and I looked at the screen.

Zeke: *No problem. I should get to sleep anyway. Long day. G'night.*

Me: *Sorry. I'd rather be with you.*

I thought that would be it, but on our way into the restaurant, I got another text.

Zeke: *Have fun. You deserve it.*

My heart melted.

Me: *I'm not exactly having fun. More of a favor for Harvey.*

Zeke: *Your lawyer?*

Me: *Yeah.*

Zeke: *Well, TRY to have fun.*

Me: *Okay. Why don't you come late tomorrow night and stay over?*

Zeke: *Sounds good. See you then.*

I blushed when I realized Marchant had been holding the door to the restaurant for me while I'd been standing by the car staring at my phone with what was probably a sappy expression. I pocketed it and gave him a smile.

"Thanks, Mr. Marchant."

His answering smile was radiant, all teeth and deep dimples. "Please, call me Tomas. Mr. Marchant makes me feel old." As we walked into the dark interior, his hand briefly came to rest on the small of my back. The move reminded me of Zeke, and I hurried my steps so Tomas's hand would fall away.

The restaurant was almost empty. The owner had kept the kitchen open late and a skeleton staff waited on us. Tomas sat close to me, his arm intimately brushing mine with every move either of us made. I knew from my time abroad that other countries didn't always have the same issues about personal space as we did in America, so I shifted in my chair, attempting to be friendly without being encouraging. I tried to add to the conversation by telling about the LGBTQ center Jon's brother was starting.

"You must be exhausted," Janine said to me as they lingered over wine, and I tried not to droop in my chair.

"I'm sorry. Long day. I thought about ordering some coffee, but I'd just have trouble falling asleep when I got home."

"No reason to be sorry," Harvey said.

"We must get you home," Tomas said, "although I confess to not wanting the night to end. I am honored to have met such an accomplished young man whom I so admire."

I smiled politely. Harvey paid the bill, and I excused myself to go to the restroom. As I was washing my hands, the door opened, and Tomas stepped in.

"Harvey and Janine are bringing the car around." He turned toward a urinal and unzipped his pants. I hesitated, not wanting to be rude by leaving the room.

"I have enjoyed myself tonight," Tomas said.

"It was a very pleasant evening," I said. He washed his hands, and we walked into the lobby.

Tomas helped me with my cashmere coat, and we stepped out onto the sidewalk as Harvey pulled up to the curb.

On the drive to my building, Harvey and Janine chatted with Tomas about business and politics while I tried my best to stay awake. I wasn't sure how Tomas could have enjoyed my company so much when I could barely keep my eyes open. When we pulled up outside my building, I quickly said my goodbyes, envisioning my bed with its new down comforter.

If I was lucky, I'd get a solid six hours sleep.

CHAPTER SEVENTEEN

Zeke

I'd been bummed I couldn't go to Morgan's Friday night and also a little jealous. As tight as Morgan's schedule was, I envied anyone who got a piece of his time.

I knew I'd thrown myself into a relationship with him, but it seemed to be working out okay. Even with our differences, we *worked*. Thinking about sleeping with him again got me fired up, and by the time Saturday night rolled around, I had a stiffy threatening to rip its way out of my pants. I couldn't wait to wrap my arms around Morgan and kiss those soft lips.

Oh, man. I had it bad.

I left the clubhouse long before Morgan was due to be home, so I could pick up something to make for dinner. He was always famished after dancing, and I worried about his eating habits, which just further proved what a goner I was for him.

I bought a newspaper while I was at it, and after putting together the salad and getting the steaks in the oven, I sat down on Morgan's couch to look through it.

By the time I'd reached the society page, I'd begun to skim. I'm not sure I would have recognized the back of Morgan's head, but the caption stood out: *Young Wentworth Heir seen out with Paris Billionaire at Gallery Opening.* And there was Morgan standing next to a swanky man in an expensive suit who reminded me of an older Clark Kent with better glasses. The way he had his hand on Morgan's back as they stood in front of some framed sketches made my blood boil. Was this Morgan's lawyer?

The Daily News said the Paris billionaire's name was *Tomas Marchant* and speculated on whether the older man, a professed

REBECCA JAMES

homosexual, was dating the young CEO and dance prodigy. I crumpled the paper in my hands. We'd never put a name to what we were doing or claimed to be exclusive, but I'd thought we were.

Had I been an idiot?

Did Morgan enjoy being fucked by a muscular biker but had other, more presentable guys to take him out to fancy events—like art galleries and cheese tasting or whatever? I could never see myself taking him to anything like that. Imagining myself crammed into a monkey suit holding a glass of champagne staring at walls full of incomprehensible doodles was downright laughable.

But you'd do it for him, my mind whispered. I would, but I knew I'd be an embarrassment to him. I didn't know anything about art. I hadn't even been to college.

Hell, what would somebody like Morgan Wentworth want with a guy like me? Of course he'd have to find somebody appropriate to take him to places like that.

And I'd taken him ice skating. He must have thought I was such a loser.

No, I told myself. Morgan had looked really happy to go skating, and you'd had a great time.

I took a deep breath and let it out before taking the steaks out of the oven. Seeing the picture of Morgan with that guy made me sick with fury, but I knew Morgan. There was an explanation. All I had to do was ask him.

I would if he ever got home. He was late. I covered the food and flopped onto the couch, telling myself over and over not to jump to conclusions. Before I realized it, I'd dozed off.

"Something smells great."

My eyes fluttered open to focus on Morgan smiling down at me. Immediately, my heart reacted by leaping around in my chest.

"Sorry I'm so late," Morgan said, leaning against the couch and running his fingers through my hair. "Erik had me practicing long after everyone else left, the sadist. I think he had it in for me because I was allowed to leave early last night." He turned and walked toward the kitchen. "Dinner's not cold, is it?"

"Shouldn't be," I said, getting up off the couch. I followed him into the kitchen. He looked sexy as hell in tight jeans and a soft gray T-shirt.

"So, you had fun last night?"

Morgan shrugged. "It was okay. I was really tired and kept thinking about bed."

I thought of the proprietary hand resting just above the swell of Morgan's ass, and I gritted my teeth.

"Zeke?"

I blinked, wondering what kind of look I'd had on my face to make Morgan appear so unsure. I pulled him to me, not rough exactly, but not gentle either. I looked down into those dark, dark eyes, searching for something. When they flared with heat, I kissed him. Morgan's hand went to the bulge in my pants, and when I pulled away, he was smiling that naughty smile of his. Jealousy and possessiveness flared in me. I'd give him what we both wanted. Putting my lips just under his ear so they brushed the sensitive skin there, I murmured, "You like it when I take you hard, don't you?" *You're mine. I'm all you need.*

Morgan's breath hitched, and his heart slammed against my chest. Ire and lust kindled deep in my belly. *Mine.*

I sucked a bruise on Morgan's neck, and he moaned, long fingers digging into my shoulders. I bit along the column of his throat, unable to tell where jealous rage ended and white-hot lust began.

You're not good enough for him, my insecure side insisted, while the more rational portion of mind who knew Morgan for who he was kept repeating, *He's not like that.*

My fingers were surprisingly steady as I unbuttoned the front of Morgan's jeans, glad that he'd changed after practice. I know I would have ripped a pair of tights in half rather than taken the time to get them off. I backed him up until he hit the kitchen table. Morgan cried out when I swung him around and yanked his pants to his ankles, but it was a cry full of lust. He grabbed hold of the table to keep himself upright as I squeezed his ass with both hands.

"Do you like it when I'm rough with you?" I asked, voice guttural with desire. *Mine.*

Morgan swallowed and nodded, and I smacked his butt, making him jump.

Leaning closer, I breathed into his ear. "Are you sure?"

He nodded again. "Yes."

"Good, because I'm going to fuck you over this table."

Morgan made a noise that had precum dripping from my aching cock. I ground my erection against his ass, denim to smooth skin.

"God, Zeke." Morgan panted as my hands wandered underneath his shirt. I twisted his nipples hard, and he cried out. With his legs spread wide, I could see his dick standing straight out from his body, leaking from the tip. That showed me better than words how much he liked what I was doing. I bet *Mr. Tomas Marchant* wouldn't fuck him like I was about to. I pushed Morgan down until his cheek pressed against the cool wood and proceeded to open him up with a spit-slick finger.

"Christ. Oh, my God." Morgan's dark eyes glazed over.

"You want me in there?" I asked, giddy at the sight of him shaking, ass tilting upward to accept more.

"God, yes."

The sound of my zipper lowering was very loud in the quiet apartment. I took out my cock, rubbing the Prince Albert against the crack of Morgan's ass. With my other hand, I held him down by the neck.

"Zeke, fuck me, please."

I loved that he wanted me so bad.

"I'm gonna split you apart," I said with a growl, and Morgan moaned, rocking up on his toes.

After seeing that photo, I wanted to brand him as mine, and Morgan blossomed under my dominance, eagerly begging with every rough swipe of my fingers inside him.

I spit into Morgan's crack and pulled his ass cheeks apart, watching the saliva run into his tiny furl. I couldn't wait to get in there. Thinking about Marchant or anyone else being in that hot hole made me crazy. Morgan was mine and only mine. I barely managed to dig a condom out of my wallet and get it on before I was pressing urgently against Morgan's tight opening.

It took everything in me to go easy while pushing the head of my cock past Morgan's sphincter, but once in, I let go, pounding into him hard and fast. Morgan yelled, holding onto the table edge, encouraging me with groans and grunts that set me aflame, and all the while I thought, how many men has Morgan been with? Had any of them satisfied him like I did?

Hooking an arm around Morgan's left leg, I lifted his knee to the table and drove in at a new angle. The tendons in my neck bulged as I slammed into him, cock swelling in the snug heat even as a voice deep inside told me my reaction to the newspaper piece was over the top.

With a sudden, blinding rush, I imploded, the strength of my climax shaking me to the core. Morgan lay beneath me, breathing hard, back slick with sweat. I reached around to jack him and found his cock spent. I'd been so charged with lust, I hadn't noticed he'd gotten off.

I helped him stand on shaking legs.

"Wow," Morgan said hoarsely, turning and nuzzling against me, fingertips running over the length of my spine under my shirt. "That was really something." He chuckled into my neck. "Can we eat now?"

"Yeah," I managed to get out before reaching for the paper towels on the counter.

When we'd cleaned up and sat down at the table, food served, I felt calm enough to broach the subject, but Morgan beat me to the punch.

"What got into you just now? You've never been that... um, intense. Not that I'm complaining, mind you." He grinned at me.

I took a sip of beer. "I guess I was a little riled up."

"You think?" Morgan smirked before taking another bite of steak.

"I saw a picture in the paper that made me go a little crazy." At Morgan's confused look, I got up and fetched the wrinkled paper, flattening it out before giving it to him. I ate my salad while he looked at it.

"This is from last night," he said. "That's Harvey's friend, Tomas. He was a little handsy, I guess, but in a fatherly way."

"I see that." When I met Morgan's gaze, he looked amused, which sparked my anger. "What?"

"You're jealous."

"Hell, yeah, I'm jealous. He's got his hand on you. Out in public."

"That was one of the few times he touched me."

I saw red. "He touched you other times?"

"We went out to dinner, the four of us. He sat close, and his arm brushed mine a lot. He admires my dancing, that's all."

I was only partially mollified and kept frowning.

"It wasn't a date, Zeke. I made sure of that before I agreed to go."

"It kind of looks like one."

"Harvey had assured me it wasn't, and Tomas didn't try to make it into one. He's a fan, and I was only helping to entertain Harvey's friend. Hell, the guy's old enough to be my father."

I put my fork down, no longer hungry. "He's a better match for you than I am."

Morgan looked up from his plate. "Where's this coming from? I know we haven't defined what we're doing, but we're sleeping together, and for me that means something."

I swallowed, unsure what to say. Morgan got up and came around the table, plopping down on my lap. My cock responded as it always does to him by getting rock hard in seconds. He kissed me.

"You know money and shit doesn't matter to me," he said.

I nodded, hands automatically running from his flat belly up to his ribs. His lips were warm and tasted of salad dressing.

"Let's go to bed, huh? I'm exhausted and just want to feel your arms wrapped around me."

I couldn't refuse him. I was bothered by what he'd told me, even if it had been meant to be reassuring, but I wanted to hold him.

This time we made love. That's the only thing to call it. I touched him everywhere, and when I entered him, our eyes met. I kept a steady, slow pace while we moved together until Morgan shattered beneath me, my name on his lips. I followed right after.

In minutes, Morgan was out like a light, but I couldn't sleep. I kept thinking about how different we were, and how I'd never be able to fit into his world. His phone buzzed where he'd left it on the nightstand, and I glanced at it. A text message showed on the locked screen.

I will be in touch soon. Looking forward to seeing you again.

CHAPTER EIGHTEEN

Morgan

After Zeke had stripped me of every thought in my head and played my body like a fine instrument, I'd sunk into a deep sleep. Sex with Zeke was always good, but between him going all cave-man on me over the kitchen table and then making love to me in bed, I'd never felt so good. I woke up smiling.

Until I realized Zeke had gone.

I grabbed my phone, ready to call him, and saw a text message on the screen.

Hell.

"Don't tell me you ran off because of that message from Tomas," I said as soon as he picked up the phone.

"I have a lot of work to do today."

"Zeke."

"Why the fuck does he have your number?"

"Harvey gave it to him because of business. He wants to buy a building."

"He wants to see you again."

"So? It's business. I'll hook him up with the proper channels, that's all."

"Maybe you should see him. Date him."

"What's that supposed to mean?" I was getting angry. I'd told Zeke he was the one I wanted to be with. Why was he being such an ass?

"It means, this Marchant guy is way more in your league than I am."

"And what fucking league is that? You're acting like a child."

"Funny thing for a child to say."

142

"Dammit, Zeke, would you stop being this way?"

"What way?"

I groaned. This wasn't getting us anywhere. "Today's my only day off, and we're not going to spend it together?"

"I told you, I got a lot to do."

"That's bullshit. You finished working on those cars so we could spend today together, and now you're in a snit because you're insecure about a text message I had absolutely no control over." When Zeke didn't say anything, I sighed. "Fine. I'll talk to you later."

I didn't have time to cater to Zeke's baby shit. This was my only day off, and if he wasn't going to spend it with me, I was going to get some things done. My refrigerator was practically empty, so I made a list and went grocery shopping.

A couple hours later, as I was unpacking the food, my phone rang. Hope bloomed until I saw the name on my screen.

"Hi, Harvey," I answered.

"Hey, I just wanted to call and tell you I'm sorry that I gave Tomas your number. He can be a little pushy, especially in business."

I pinched the bridge of my nose between finger and thumb. "It's fine. No worries. Really."

"Okay. I just felt badly about it, especially after Janine chewed me out."

We both laughed. "It's really not a problem. Forget it."

When I hung up with Harvey, I sagged against the counter. Being in an argument with Zeke sucked. I didn't get why he was so upset. Tomas hadn't really done anything untoward, and I wasn't convinced he was interested in anything other than a business relationship. Even if he were, so what? I didn't want him. You didn't see me asking Zeke if that girl had been back, trying to suck his dick again. Thinking about that made me angry. With a huff of frustration, I went to take a shower and stood under the hot water until my skin turned red. When I stepped out, I looked at my blank phone screen. I wanted Zeke to call me back and apologize, but obviously, he wasn't going to do that today.

Deciding to continue to use my time wisely rather than sit around and mope, I sent a text to Gerald Peters to meet me at Wentworth Building and got dressed.

CHAPTER NINETEEN

Morgan

"We aren't discriminatory," Gerald said. "We never fired Guy Germane."

"No, you just kept him from moving up or from working in his preferred area of expertise. Still discrimination, Gerald," I said.

I was pissed. We sat in what had once been my father's office, which I'd never officially taken over, and I could tell Peters was not happy I'd chosen the location for this meeting or that I was sitting at the chair behind the desk.

After I'd sent a text to Peters telling him I wanted to meet, I'd taken an Uber to Wentworth building. While waiting for him in my dad's office, I'd caught up on my emails and read one from an employee, Guy Germane, who claimed his gay marriage had kept him from succeeding in his job. He said he'd spoken to Peters about it on more than one occasion, along with HR, but nothing had ever been done. He was considering legal action. I'd immediately called him, and by the time I'd gotten off the phone, a plan was forming in my mind.

I now shared that plan with Gerald. "I'm promoting him from Assistant VP of Marketing and Brand Development to VP of Agency Leasing."

The veins on Peters' forehead stood out like a road map. "That would be a big mistake."

"My biggest mistake has been trusting you to run everything properly," I said. "We need someone like Germane in Agency Leasing."

"By putting that man in direct contact with clients, you're risking alienating some of our most conservative and lucrative customers. You're going against everything Allen built this company for."

I bristled. "Whether my father was a bigot or not doesn't matter to me. I'm not one, and I'm not going to allow *my company* to discriminate. And I'd advise you to think before you speak. Are you aware I'm gay?"

Peters blanched.

"I'll take that as a no and assume you now understand that I will not change my mind. Are we clear on this?"

My facade of confidence was wearing thin, but faced with breaking or becoming stronger, I would choose the latter.

Peters gave me a hard stare. "This isn't going to go over well with the board."

"What, my sexuality or my choice to promote an openly gay man? Perhaps it's time I bought out those on the board who don't agree with me."

Gerald shook his head. "You're just a kid. You don't know what you're doing. Albert Easter—"

"If you can't think of a way to keep an important client other than to cater to his discriminatory views, leave Albert Easter to me. I want you to call a board meeting as soon as possible."

A sneer pulled at Gerald's upper lip. "If I do, are you going to be able to fit it into your dance schedule?"

I leaned forward, hands planted firmly on my father's desk. *My desk.* "Let me worry about that. And from here on out, Gerald, you'd do well to remember I'm *the kid, the dancer, and the queer* who signs your paychecks."

I held my stance until Peters stomped out of the office, then sagged back into the chair. My body was tired and sore, as always, but my mind was running on overdrive. I knew the steps I was taking were huge, but they felt right. But I needed advice.

After typing out an email to Germane that I wanted to meet with him in person, I pulled up Tomas Marchant's number on my phone.

☙❧

Three weeks zipped by. Tomas Marchant had been more than happy to meet with me several nights a week after my rehearsals to answer my questions. We met at restaurants in back booths and ate while I peppered him with questions. He'd been extremely helpful, and as I learned more of the ins and outs of corporate business, I was surprised at how interesting I found it and how much I wanted to incorporate what I was learning. At Tomas' urging, I signed up for online business classes.

The rest of my time was a blur of dancing, sleeping, and trying to get Zeke to text more than a few words to me. He'd made every excuse possible not to see me. Although my days were full and didn't allow me any time to wallow, at night in bed Zeke appeared in my dreams, making love to me like he had that last time. The dreams were so real, I sometimes awoke thinking he was in bed beside me. Then reality would slam into me like a train, and I would drag myself to the Arts center to begin another exhausting day.

Zeke claimed he had a lot of cars to work on. He never answered my calls but would text, usually to say he'd call me later, which he never did.

Tomas left for Paris for a few days, and when he returned, he called to ask me to meet him for lunch. We agreed he'd pick me up, and we would eat someplace close to the Arts Center.

When we'd disconnected, I laid my head on Nikki's shoulder. She'd come by to catch some time with me after rehearsal. My feet ached, and the rest of me felt like a limp noodle.

"I'm so tired."

"Want me to leave so you can go to bed?"

"No. I mean, I'm always exhausted."

"Who was that on the phone?"

I yawned. "Tomas Marchant. I told you he's been helping me with business stuff."

She nodded. "Nice of him. An important businessman taking time out to mentor a young guy. Are you sure he doesn't have another kind of interest in you?"

I frowned. "I wasn't sure at first, but he hasn't made any advances. He seems to look at me like a son."

She raised her brows. "Really? Well, that's... nice. I'm glad he's helping you out. I know you've been excited to learn more about your company."

I nodded, fighting another yawn. "It's been great. I never thought I'd get into it so much."

"I don't know how you have the time."

I groaned. "I don't either. I just cram it in, giving up sleep." I looked at Nikki. "I don't know what I want anymore."

She patted my leg. "You don't have to figure it all out right now."

I leaned my head back and stared at the ceiling. "I've always wanted to dance. Always. And now I'm so close to being accepted into a company, and I feel like it's all too much. What's wrong with me?"

"Nothing's wrong with you. If you decide you don't want to dance, you don't have to do it. And if you decide you do want to, but not in a dance company, that's fine, too."

My competitive nature balked at those words. I felt as though if I were going to dance, I had to go for the gold. Dance in a company. Become a soloist, then a principal dancer. That had always been the plan.

But I had to be honest with myself. I just wasn't sure I wanted to devote my life to achieve that anymore. So, what was my dream now? To run Wentworth Properties?

"What about Zeke?" Nikki asked.

I continued staring at the ceiling. "What about him?"

"Are you guys over?"

I closed my eyes. "God, I hope not. He hasn't said so, but he's avoiding me. I'm trying to give him space, but... maybe this is his way of letting me down easy."

"Easy?" Nikki exploded, causing my eyes to fly open at her outburst. She stood up. "Leaving your place because of a stupid text, stringing you along, refusing to tell you to your face what he's thinking—that makes things *easy*?" She shook her head. "Easy for him, more like. He's being a colossal prick."

I couldn't argue with that. But what good did anger do? I'd been given the principal male role in *Cinderella*, and I was juggling that while trying to keep on top of Wentworth Properties. I was fucking exhausted all the time. I knew I wasn't eating well, but I wasn't hungry. My pizza sat untouched on my plate, the vegetables beginning to take on a waxy look that turned my stomach.

As far as Wentworth Properties went, I was fairly pleased with my progress. After announcing at the last board meeting my refusal to tolerate discrimination of any kind, I'd bought out two board members. If my father hadn't had Peters and the others sign a non-compete agreement at the beginning, I felt sure Gerald Peters would be threatening to leave and take our clients with him. As it was, he just took every opportunity to let me know he didn't agree with my decisions. Remembering my impression back when I was sixteen that he was somehow threatened by me, I wondered. Was he just a controlling dick who wanted to be top dog, or was it something more dangerous? I'd quietly hired someone to look into the business dealings in the past three years and awaited their answer. If Peters wasn't clean as a whistle, he was out.

"Are you going to go to go see Zeke in person and make him talk to you, or are you going to sulk for the rest of your life?" Nikki asked, throwing away our trash.

I rubbed my eyes. "I was kind of waiting for him to come apologize to me."

"How's that working out for ya?" Nikki turned and crossed the room to pick up something from the floor. "What's this? Did somebody shove it under the door? It wasn't there when I came in." She handed me the folded piece of paper.

I unfolded it. Letters cut from a magazine underscored the malicious feel of the message.

Better stick with what you know, ballerina boy. Doing otherwise could be bad for your health.

"*Ballerina boy* is an oxymoron," I muttered even as a chill ran up my back.

Reading over my shoulder, Nikki gasped. "What the hell?" She snatched it out of my hands. "This is a threat! Oh, my God, Morgan, who would be threatening you? Call the police."

I shook my head. "It's a disgruntled board member. Probably Gerald Peters. He says Albert Easter's been making noise about the LBGTQ center opening near one of his furniture stores, and a lot of the shareholders are worried. It's freaking him out, and he's trying to bully me."

"So, he *threatens* you?"

"They want me to sell out. Most of them, anyway. They think of me as a kid they can scare off." But lately, I'd gotten the feeling a few board members were coming around and maybe even approving of the changes I was making. Germane was proving to be very good at his new job, and we hadn't heard a peep from Albert Easter, despite Peters' warnings.

Nikki shook her head. "Fuck. Have you gotten any other threats?"

"Not any that blatant," I said. Besides the car that had followed me home, I'd received a few hang-up calls, the numbers blocked. "Don't worry about it."

"How can I not worry?" Nikki looked like she was about to cry, but I was too tired to comfort her. Maybe I had a cold coming on, or the flu. *Great, just what I need. I don't have time to be sick.*

"Morgan, I'm so sorry all this is happening to you. First Zeke dumps you, then you get all this hate..." she left off, brows lowered in worry.

"He hasn't dumped me. You're not making me feel better, you know." I attempted a smile.

She shook her head. "You're unbelievable."

Nikki left after making me promise I'd let her know of any more threats, veiled or otherwise. Exhausted, I fell into bed and didn't wake until the alarm on my phone went off signaling it was time for another grueling day.

CHAPTER TWENTY
Zeke

The morning after I left Morgan's place in a huff about that prick Marchant's text, I walked into the garage of the clubhouse to find an unexpected visitor.

"Hey, Zeke."

"Pop. What are you doing here?" The old fear rose but didn't grab hold. My father looked old and tired.

"I've been looking for you." My old man leaned against the wall and surveyed the two cars I was currently working on while I briefly considered and dismissed lowering the garage door on him.

"Heard you got yourself quite a little business," he said.

I didn't move from where I stood on the three steps leading down into the garage from the house. "I do all right. Why've you been looking for me?"

"Hadn't heard from you in a while."

That was an understatement. I might have laughed if I hadn't been so wary. I waited for whatever he had to say because no way did Pop come looking for me because he missed me.

"You ran off before I could talk to you at Steve's funeral. You sure grew up, Son." Pop's eyes roamed over me appraisingly, and I fought not to squirm as I had as a kid. "Been taking care of yourself. Lifting weights, looks like."

"I do all right," I said again, thinking of the million and one times he'd told me I was scrawny when I was a kid. I noticed his muscle tone wasn't all that impressive. Either he'd lost a lot of it, or my mind had remembered his physique as something more than it really had been.

Pop chuckled. "Never had much to say, did ya? Okay, I'll get to the point. Thing is, I'm starting up a garage of my own. I've been wanting to for years, and I'm finally in a place where I can make it happen. I want you to come work with me."

If, life on the line, I'd had to make a list of the top five reasons my old man would show up, I'd never have come up with that one.

I listened, stunned, as he kept talking.

"I've been saving up, and when your Uncle Terry passed a few months ago, he left me enough that I could make the down payment on a place I'd had my eye on over in Queens. Gonna call it *Ivers and Son Car Maintenance.*"

"And you want me to work with you?" Anger stirred. After telling me time and time again that I'd never make something of myself, he suddenly showed up asking me to go into business with him? I wanted to rail at him. Ask him how a stupid, pathetic little cunt like his youngest son could possibly be the business partner he wanted. But something held me off.

"Of course, *you,*" Pop said. "See any other sons around here?"

I crossed my arms over my chest. "What about Pete?"

My father scoffed. "Pete's not here, plus he was never any good with his hands. You're the one who got my talent for tinkering. At least, that's what I hear. Why didn't you ever tell me you were interested in mechanics? All those times I showed you stuff, you never opened your mouth. Hell, imagine my surprise when I start hearing recommendations for a Zeke Ivers out in Clinton Hill who has a real knack for fixing cars."

Something warm bloomed in my chest at the praise.

I should tell him to go fuck himself. That I was doing fine on my own and didn't need him. But the little boy inside me who'd always wanted his father's love and attention wouldn't allow the words past my lips.

"I don't know," I said.

Pop ran a hand through his thick hair, which was mostly gray now. Way more than it had been at Steve's funeral. "The place'll be yours when I die."

I was a good mechanic. A real good one. But I'd never have the chance to have my own place like he was talking about. Not without a miracle.

Maybe that's what this was.

151

THE BALLERINO AND THE BIKER

"My home is here now," I said, just in case he had any ideas of my moving back home with him. That wasn't happening.

"I'm not asking you to go anywhere, just to run the business with me. What d'ya say?"

My eyes locked with Pop's, and I saw something there I never thought I'd see: behind the tough exterior was vulnerability.

"Come in and have a beer," I said, pushing open the door to the house.

Pop walked past me and looked around the inside of the club like everyone who first sees it does. They expect something rougher or more like TV when it's really just a house.

"What's this MC about?" Pop asked. "You're not into anything illegal, are you?"

Anger reared. "Leave the club out of this," I said sharply.

The way Pop looked at me — with something close to respect in his eyes — made me realize I'd never stood up to him before. Not once. My chest swelled with emotion, filling the yawning emptiness that had taken up inside me since I'd argued with Morgan. I knew I should make things right with him, but my pride wouldn't let me. God, I missed him. His absence festered within me like an open wound.

Pop accepted the beer I handed him and popped it open.

"You really got a place?" I asked, pulling a chair out with my foot and sitting down. Pop sat across from me, a grin splitting his worn face.

"Sure do. Three garages and plenty of room in the office. You gotta come see it."

I fiddled with the piercing in my tongue. "If I do this, I want a legal contract."

"I got no problem with that. We'll iron it all out."

I'd never seen the old man look so excited about something. I'd never known he'd wanted his own garage. Hell, it wasn't like he'd ever discussed his hopes and dreams with any of us. Seeing him like this now was weird. Like I was looking at a different version of my pop. It loosened something inside me, and I wasn't sure if that was a good or bad thing.

But the lure of owning a place was overwhelming. Even if I had to co-own it with a jerk like my old man, I would be setting myself up for the rest of my life. I wouldn't be going nowhere like I had been. I leaned back in my chair, hoping I wasn't making a huge mistake.

"Tell me about it."

ନ୍ଧେ

That night, after driving to the place with Pop, I discussed his proposition with Blaze and Dante. They knew my issues with my family, and I appreciated their caution. The place was larger and nicer than I'd anticipated, and excitement had sparked within me when I'd seen it. I trusted my best friends to let me know if the whole idea was crazy and tried to be patient through their questions.

Dante put down the copy of the contract we'd been going over and turned his deep blue gaze on me.

"Is it something you really want? A business, I mean?"

"Let's put it this way; if it weren't for my pop being part of the equation, I'd be jumping all over this." I stubbed out my cigarette in the ashtray on the coffee table.

Blaze studied me for a moment. "You're grown now, Zeke. Bigger than your old man. Stronger than him. Hell, you've always been smarter than him. If you really want this, I know you can handle it. And the place'll be yours when he's dead and gone. Besides, this might give you some closure on things that have been left hanging too long."

I met his eyes and nodded. He knew better than anybody how messed up I'd been when I'd left home. I wanted this. Pop had no power over me anymore, and maybe doing this would drown those voices of the past in my head.

You'll own your own business, my subconscious told me. But even that wouldn't put me on Morgan's level, I reminded myself. I wasn't good enough for him and never would be.

Morgan had his whole life ahead of him and deserved more than a nobody like me who'd only bring him down. I should ignore his texts like I had been his calls, or better yet, I should grow some balls and break things off with him. But every time Morgan sent me a text, my heart thumped out of my chest, and I had to answer, even if only a few terse words. And, *dammit*, I couldn't bring myself to officially end things.

But lately, Morgan's texts were getting fewer and farther between. Maybe he was moving on. Maybe I was turning out to be as easy to forget as I'd imagined.

I called my old man and told him I was in.

"What's up with Swish?" I asked as we cleared our dinner plates.

Dante glanced toward the back porch where Swish had remained grooming a small, flat-faced dog rather than coming in to eat with us.

"He's got his panties in a wad about something," Dante said.

I didn't push. Something was up between Dante and Swish, but I wasn't going to spend the time trying to figure it out. I headed out to the garage and started gathering up my tools. Pop was going to be there soon, and I'd signed the contract. I was doing this.

Excitement stirred in my belly, and I started whistling as I worked. It caught me off guard when someone shoved me from behind. It wasn't much of a shove, but I swung around, ready to fight, only to freeze when I saw Morgan's friend Nikki standing there looking at me like I was shit on her shoe. I'd been so deep in my thoughts, I hadn't even heard her car.

I dumped the tools I was holding into the open steel box I'd drug off the bottom shelf and wiped my hand on a rag. "What are you doin' here?"

"I came to tell you what a sorry son-of-a-bitch you are," Nikki said.

I should have expected it. In fact, I was surprised she hadn't come sooner. "Well, go ahead and do it and get outta here. I've got work to do."

She backed up a step, so I wasn't towering over her. Not for the first time, she reminded me of an angry little chihuahua. Well, she was yapping at a junkyard dog who wasn't in the mood for her sticking her nose into things.

She narrowed her amber eyes at me. "You're really something, you know that?"

"Don't you think Morgan's old enough to fight his own battles? You gotta come out here and do it for him?"

"I'm all he's got, you ass, and I want to know why the hell you're being such a shit to him."

I sighed. "I don't have time for this."

Nikki looked like she wanted to hit me. Her nostrils flared, and she curled her fists. "Make time."

She was really pissing me off, or maybe I was just transferring my anger at myself to her, or some Freudian shit like that. Either way, I wanted her out of my face. But she wasn't done.

"You're just one more in a long list of people who have left him." Nikki raised both hands and shoved me again, this time harder, managing to knock me back a step before I could recover. Her words hit like a blade to my heart. Hurting Morgan was the last thing I wanted to do.

"If you don't want to be with him, at least have the decency to tell him, asshole."

The sound of footfalls made us both turn. My old man rounded the corner and looked curiously at us. He must have parked in the back.

Nikki sent me one more scathing look and hiked her purse strap onto her shoulder. "End it like a man. Morgan deserves better than to be left wondering about a virginity-stealing, chicken shit, ass-wipe like you." She turned and stomped across the yard to where her car was parked on the street.

I stood staring after her, mouth open.

What was she talking about, virginity-stealing? Hell, she'd been the one to take Morgan's virginity. Unless... she was talking about his virginity with a man. But no. I hadn't been Morgan's first guy.

Had I?

With a squeal of tires, Nikki pulled her Nissan from the curb and sped off down the street.

I turned to Pop who was looking at me with bemusement.

"I take it Morgan's her best friend."

I momentarily panicked before realizing my father thought Morgan was a girl. I started to nod, to take the easy way out. Let him think what he wanted. Pop didn't have to know what I'd done. Morgan and I were probably finished anyway.

I don't want us to be finished.

The image of Morgan's beautiful face rose in my mind, and so much love swelled within me, I thought I was going to slam to the ground under the weight of it.

Hell, no. Pop isn't going to take Morgan from me. Even if all I've got left is a memory.

Ire rising within me, I crossed my arms over my chest and leaned back against the tool bench. If Pop was going to back out of this, let him back out now.

"Yeah. Morgan's her best friend. And he's a guy. What do you think about that? Your scrawny son who caused you so much embarrassment is the faggot you always claimed he was."

I watched Pop's face harden and his jaw start to work back and forth. Once such a familiar sight, it now gave me chills. But I wasn't thirteen anymore.

"That's right, Pop. I like cock. Still want me to be the son in *Ivers and Son?* Maybe your best bet's with Pete after all."

Disgust mingled with something else settled on my old man's face. I turned away from him and began unloading the tools from the container.

"What are you doing?" Pop said.

"I spent the better part of my childhood and adolescence trying to live up to what you wanted in a son. A minute ago I thought about lying about the most important person in my life. I'm not going back to that. You can run the place alone."

Pop's tone turned oddly plaintive. "What do you mean? You said you were in. I ain't got that many years left in me. I want my name to live on."

I sighed and straightened, still facing away from him.

"I'm in love with a man, and I'm not going to pretend otherwise. Not for you, not for anybody." I took a breath and turned around, determined to face my father's disgust.

It was there, but so was something else. Fear. Surprised, I froze. Pop didn't want to do this alone. He needed me.

"Zeke." Pop ran his hand over his reddened face. It looked like it was taking an enormous effort for him to say the words. "What you do in the privacy of your own home is your business. I'm talking about running a business together. That's all."

I narrowed my eyes, confused. What was he playing at? "Aren't you going to call me names? Fudge-packer? Pillow-biter? Sissy? Come on. You always had plenty of them. I'm telling you outright I like cock, and you're willing to overlook it?"

My old man shifted his gaze to the yard and beyond.

I pressed on. "You want me to go into business with you so bad, you're willing to just ignore I'm bisexual?"

REBECCA JAMES

That got his attention. "So, you do like women."

"That's not the point. I'm in love with a man. Are you saying you're willing to let that go and work with me?"

My father swallowed before giving a stiff nod. This was costing him; I could tell.

I shook my head as relief flooded through me. "You must really want this."

"Running a garage is my dream. We all got 'em."

"Yeah. We do."

Something within me shifted and settled.

The minute I got the chance, I was calling Morgan. Maybe it wasn't impossible. Maybe we could make it work.

CHAPTER TWENTY-ONE

Morgan

Tomas surprised me by paying a cafe owner to close shop for the morning so we could have the place to ourselves. It was over the top and ridiculous, but that seemed to be Tomas Marchant in a nutshell.

I was still flying on happiness after Zeke's call early that morning. I'd dropped a coffee cup when his name had appeared on my phone screen. The sound of his voice had had me gripping the counter edge in my kitchen as for one, terrifying moment, I'd thought he'd called to officially end things.

But, voice soft and relaxed, Zeke had told me he was sorry for everything. That he missed me and wanted to see me but had to finish something up first. He'd tell me all about it later, hopefully tomorrow.

I still didn't know what to make of it.

I'd listened to my voice mail on the way to rehearsal and had three more hang-up calls plus a heavy breather. I'd erased them all. Peters wasn't going to force me out of my own company, and I refused to let anything ruin my day.

"You didn't have to ask the owner to close the shop," I said to Tomas as we took off our coats in the quiet interior.

"You deserve a quiet place to recharge," Tomas said. "Besides, I don't want any interruptions while you tell me how your last meeting with Peters went."

I had to admit not being in a crowd felt good. I drank from a bottle of water and slipped my sore feet out of my boots before propping them on the chair in front of me. As I covered a pepper cracker in Brie, I told him about my last meeting with Peters.

"He seemed surprised at my knowledge," I said with a smirk.

"As we'd hoped," Tomas said and winked.

I stuffed another Brie-covered cracker into my mouth. I hadn't realized how hungry I was, but thinking back, I hadn't had anything since the energy shake I'd made at six A.M. after Zeke's phone call.

Tomas looked amused. "You should take better care of yourself. You're starved and look like you haven't slept in a week."

"I expect to sleep well tonight."

"Oh?" Tomas opened a bottle of sparkling water. "Why is that?"

"My boyfriend and I have been through a rough patch, but it's ironed out now."

Tomas smiled. "If he makes you happy, that's good. Please keep your health in mind always, Morgan. You are worth it."

"Thanks." I sat back. "And thank you, so much, for helping me with the business. You don't know how much I appreciate it. You're — well, let's just say you've filled a space in my life that's been empty a long time."

Tomas smiled. "I'm glad. You will make a wonderful CEO, Morgan. You have a knack for it."

My insides warmed.

"Did you speak with Darren about the buildings you wanted to look at?" I asked him after another cracker.

A small frown line divided Tomas' dark eyes just behind his custom-made Matsuda eyeglasses. "Yes. He is going to take me to see them on Tuesday of next week." He bit into a pepper cracker covered in pâté and licked the crumbs off his full bottom lip.

"Did I ever tell you I'd been to your parents' home?" he asked after a moment.

"No. When was that?"

"I was in my twenties. They were quite a bit older than I. It was when I was living here while trying to get my business off the ground in America. I went to a cocktail party there with Harvey. Your father was a smart businessman, and I appreciated his words of advice."

I thought about that as I popped a manzanilla olive stuffed with anchovies into my mouth and slathered Brie on yet another cracker.

"What were they like back then?"

Tomas cocked his head. "Cordial, welcoming."

"Was my father as driven as I remember?"

Tomas appeared to think about it. "I suppose he was, yes. I'm sure he would be very proud of everything you're doing."

I washed my food down with water. I wasn't sure if my father would be proud of me or not, but it was nice of Tomas to say so. I smiled at him and tried some smoked salmon and caviar on a cucumber slice and moaned at the explosion of flavors. Delicious.

"Has the LGBTQ center you mentioned the night of our dinner opened yet? Where is it again?" Tomas asked.

I told him, adding, "No, it hasn't opened yet, but it will be soon. They've been painting the inside. I really wish I could volunteer there in some capacity. Dance doesn't allow me any free time."

"You are a slave to your art," Tomas said. "Well, one day, after you've danced your fill, perhaps you will gain the time you desire."

I kind of hated the idea that half my life would be over by then. I could see it melting away before me, days of nothing but dance stretching out until I was too old to do it anymore. When had I started looking at my dream that way?

"Do you think that would be possible?"

I'd zoned out.

"Sorry, what?"

Tomas smiled indulgently, and the passing thought I could be sitting here with my father, sharing lunch and talking of my aspirations warmed me with a sense of family I hadn't had in a long while.

"I wondered if you would show me the LGBTQ center. I'm very interested. I've even thought about starting one or two in another needful area."

Excitement sparked, as it always did when I thought of the center and its possibilities to help kids. "Would you really be interested in doing that?"

Tomas' dimples flashed. "Certainement. I am very curious to see the building and what your friend has done with it. I think it is a very worthy cause."

"Gabe—that's the friend who's doing it—is out of town, but I could show it to you, although it would probably have to be late at night, as usual." I wanted to show it to Zeke, too. Very much. My stomach fluttered at the thought of being with him again.

"No hurry, although I'm excited to see it." Tomas chuckled. "We are like a couple of vampires, always meeting when the moon is high."

I had to smile at that. Poor Tomas had had a lot of late nights out lately because of me.

"Here." Tomas pushed more cucumber toward me. "Eat some vegetables. They are full of B-5 and omega-3 fatty acids."

I did, thinking how great it would be if Tomas really did open an LGBTQ center — maybe several of them. "There's such a need for these centers," I said. "So many homeless youths are LGBTQ."

Tomas' eyes sparkled. "You don't have to convince me; I'm in."

I began listing the programs Jon's brother had told me about the last time he visited Jon at rehearsals, and before I knew it, the rest of my lunch hour had flown by.

"Erik is going to be so angry," I said as Tomas drove me back to the center. I was late.

"I wouldn't worry. Brainard knows what a jewel he has in you."

I shook my head. "He doesn't play favorites. I've been late before, and when Erik tells him..."

"Morgan. You must become more aware of your worth. He watched you as a student in Milan and recruited you as an apprentice. Even if you didn't have such marvelous talent, you hold a lot of weight in this city."

I glanced at him, frowning. "That's not how I want to get things accomplished."

"Sometimes you must use what is available to you. There's no shame in that."

I zipped up my puffy coat and pulled on my gloves. As soon as Tomas braked, I jumped out of the rented sports car, anxious to get inside. "Thanks for lunch, Tomas. I'll text you as soon as I can get some time," I said before closing the car door. He rolled down the window.

"Oui. Do not wear yourself into the ground, mon petit garçon." He waved as I headed into the building.

It was only after I'd slipped into rehearsal without being seen and began stretching at the barre that I realized Tomas had called me his little boy.

C3&O

"Going to tell me why you're in such a good mood?" Nikki asked as she walked past me into my apartment, two chef salads in her hands.

"All in due time," I called out on the way to my room to change while Nikki got out plates and forks.

"Thanks for this," I said when I returned, taking a seat across from her. "I didn't expect to see you again so soon."

She gnawed on her bottom lip. "Yeah, well, I did something that's probably going to piss you off."

I braced myself. "What?"

"I might have gone over to the clubhouse yesterday and laid into Zeke about how he's treated you."

I groaned. "Why?"

Nikki's guilty expression morphed into indignant anger on my behalf. "Because he's a dick, and you deserve better. It infuriates me that he led you on the way he did." She paused, uncertainty creeping into her eyes. "Are you mad at me?"

I sighed. "I'd be furious if it obviously hadn't done some good. He called me early this morning before I left for rehearsal and apologized."

Nikki blinked a few times. "Wow. I didn't expect that. He didn't act like he was listening to me." She grinned. "I guess that's the reason for the happy look."

I knew the smile stretching my face was goofy as hell. "Yeah."

"Well, I know something else. A man arrived while I was there. An older man who looked a lot like Zeke. Had to be his dad."

I thought about that. "They're estranged."

She shrugged. "Could have been an uncle or something, I guess."

We finished eating, and I told her to hang out while I folded laundry. Exhausted as I was, I was wound up and not ready to go to sleep yet. She sat on my bed and helped me.

"What did you say to Zeke about me?" I imagined him in the clubhouse garage, probably wearing a tank top that showed off his muscular chest, shoulders, and arms. And no coat, of course. Which had me thinking how warm his body always was. I shivered, wishing fervently the hours would melt away so I could see him. I folded the last towel and took the pile to the hall closet. When I returned, I flung myself down beside Nikki.

"I just told him he was a prick and left. That's all I had time for before his dad, or whoever, walked over."

My eyes began to droop.

Nikki crawled off the bed. Dimly, I heard her straightening the room. A moment later, I felt a blanket fall over me where I lay sprawled on my bed.

"I'll get out of here, Morgs," she whispered in my ear before kissing my forehead. "Get some sleep."

I grunted my goodbye, knowing she'd lock the door when she left.

CB&O

It could have been minutes or hours later when I awakened to my phone ringing on the nightstand. Nikki must have set it there, because the last time I remembered having it was in the kitchen when I got home.

"Hello?" My voice sounded as groggy as I felt. I rolled over and squinted at the digital alarm clock beside my bed. 1:37 A.M.

"Morgan, this is Tomas. I'm so sorry to wake you, *mon petit*, but I am worried about your LGBTQ center."

I immediately became more awake and sat up, worn-out muscles protesting to the sudden movement. "What are you talking about?"

"I was curious after we talked today. I kept thinking about the center, and how I could open up a few myself. I worked late, as I often do, and after leaving my office, decided to take a drive to get a look at the outside. I could be mistaken, but I thought I saw some movement behind one of the upper windows. Should there be anyone there?"

Alarm shot through me. "No. Definitely not. Did you call the police?" I stood, momentarily surprised I was still in my clothes before I remembered Nikki covering me up before she left. I thought of calling Gabe, then remembered he was out of town for a few days for a rest before opening the center.

"I considered that, but I wondered if you would want them coming out here."

I'd told him about Albert Easter. And there were other clients, too, who might not appreciate the center drawing drama to the area.

"Where are you now?" I asked.

"I'm sitting in my car watching the place." Tomas's voice turned regretful. "It may be nothing, Morgan. I'm sorry I woke you, and after telling you just this afternoon you needed your sleep."

"No, it's okay. You know how much the center means to me. Could you — would you mind coming to get me? I'd feel better seeing for myself."

Could there be vandals? Again, I thought of calling the police, but what if Tomas had been mistaken? Or what if a homeless person had broken in? The temperature was in the single digits. I didn't want to call the police on someone like that.

"Of course. I'm on my way."

I was waiting downstairs when Tomas pulled up in his rental car. I hurried from the building and slipped onto the warmth of the heated seat.

"I'm sorry, Morgan. The more I think about this, the more I regret waking you. I should have called the police."

"No, I'm glad you didn't. I've had some sleep, and I really want to see if something's going on. I would hate the place to be vandalized so close to opening. Gabe's already got a list of kids waiting to move in."

Tomas pulled into traffic, and I wondered if I should call Jon. I hated to wake him if it turned out to be nothing, and he couldn't do anything about it anyway. He'd only call Gabe, and if it was a false alarm, Gabe would worry for nothing and maybe even cut his trip short. I glanced at Tomas. He was dressed as he'd been for lunch and appeared just as fresh. I didn't know how he managed it. In comparison, I had to look a mess in the sweatpants and wrinkled shirt I'd pulled from a drawer when I'd gotten home from dance.

When we parked outside the building, all appeared quiet.

"Perhaps I was wrong," Tomas said, as we stared up at the two-story corner building. Nothing seemed amiss.

"Wait, did you see that?" Tomas leaned over me to stare out the passenger window.

"What?"

"That window, there." He pointed to the second floor. I'm certain I saw movement. Do you suppose it could be a cat or other animal?"

I didn't want to get the police out there for a cat. I unbuckled my seat belt. "Let's check it out."

Tomas reached into the glove compartment and pulled out a handgun. At my shocked look, he said, "Just to be safe. I have a license."

I had to admit the gun made me feel better.

I unlocked the door to the building with the rainbow banner running down the side window and the smell of fresh paint assaulted my nose as we walked in. I turned on the lights. The main room with its colorful paintings on the wall and long information desk in the corner appeared untouched. We stood for several moments listening in the silence.

"I will check upstairs," Tomas said, and I didn't argue. He had the gun. I watched him move quietly up the staircase, his footfalls loud in the silence.

When I could no longer see him, I looked around. The place had been transformed since I'd seen it last, the formerly dark, dreary interior now bright, cheery, and welcoming. I couldn't wait to see it filled with kids in need. The floor above my head creaked as Tomas walked from room to room upstairs. Presently, he returned, pushing the gun into the pocket of his coat.

He looked chagrined. "No one up there, not even a cat or raccoon. I checked everywhere. I—"

I held up my hand. "Please don't apologize again. Since we're here, why don't I take you on that tour? I'm excited at how great it looks."

"It really does look good," Tomas agreed.

The downstairs included three living-area type rooms, one with a computer area and library, a kitchen and laundry area, and non-gender-specific restrooms.

"Gabe has several fund-raising events coming up," I told Tomas. "As you can imagine, it will take a lot of money to keep this place going. I've made a large donation." I glanced at him.

Tomas chuckled and his hand touched my lower back as we navigated our way into the next room.

"And I would be happy to do so, also. Such a good cause. How many youths will be able to stay here?"

"I think Gabe said twenty full-time, but there will be after-school programs and many other educational resources that can include so many more."

I imagined myself giving a talk to the kids on ballet, perhaps in league with Global, but when would I have the time?

"The upstairs looks good, too, although I was too preoccupied searching for an intruder to get a good look. Would you like to go up?" Tomas asked.

"Yeah, I'm dying to see the bedrooms."

I followed him up the wide staircase past a landing with a small window, the cracked glass of which had been replaced with rainbow stained glass since the last time I'd been there. A small brass plaque beneath proclaimed the stained glass had been donated by Global Ballet. We continued up another flight to the second floor, and I switched on the hall light.

While a couple walls had been knocked out downstairs to provide roomy areas for various activities, those upstairs had been divided into two or three to provide the optimal amount of sleeping space.

I gazed around at the donated bunk beds and dressers all assembled into welcoming sleep areas.

"It makes me so happy to see this all coming together," I said.

As I stood looking at the homey touches that had been added to the next room we entered, Tomas' hands settled on my shoulders.

"You are a good person, Morgan."

The compliment buoyed me, and I suddenly realized how much I'd missed having an older person in my life to give me approving words. Tomas knew so much about the business world and had helped me a lot. With him as a mentor, I could make real headway in my company. Had my father lived, I doubted he would have been as attentive.

"What are you thinking about?" Tomas asked. "You look so solemn."

"I was thinking about how helpful you've been and how good it feels to have your approval," I said honestly, blushing a little. Tomas's fingers squeezed into my shoulders, and I leaned back into the touch, so intent on comparing Tomas to my father, that it came as a jolting shock when Tomas pressed his lips to the side of my throat.

I stiffened. "Um..."

Tomas turned me to face him. Dressed all in black, he stood out ominously against the white walls of the center. A shiver ran down my spine, and I stepped back to put some space between us.

"Tomas, I..."

"It's all right, Morgan. I know what you need."

Behind the expensive glasses, Tomas' hazel eyes flickered over my face before he leaned in and kissed me, his mouth possessively rough. I didn't move, didn't respond, shocked and unable to believe I'd misjudged his intentions so badly. When he let me go, my lips throbbed, and Tomas was breathing erratically. In that moment, all his sophisticated panache slipped away, revealing something frighteningly intense underneath.

"I told you I visited your home with Harvey," Tomas said, warm breath drifting over my face, "but not that I saw you. This was before they sent you away. You were a charming boy, with such expressive eyes. I've dreamed of those eyes so many times since." He stroked underneath my jaw with his thumb, his words forming a ball of ice in the pit of my stomach. My mind was having trouble connecting the dots.

"Tomas..."

He cut me off, tone low and soothing, but also urgent in a way that scared me. "The next time I visited, your parents had sent you to Milan. It became important to me to keep up with you, make sure you were all right. I attended as many of your performances I could fit into my schedule."

Perhaps that was why he'd looked familiar to me.

"You have such a beautiful body, Morgan. Graceful, strong."

Unsettled by Tomas's words as much as his alarming change of behavior, I sought a way out of the dangerous position I'd unknowingly put myself in.

Keeping my voice as calm as I could, I said, "Maybe we should go. It's awfully late."

Tomas' gaze drank in my features. "We just got here." His hands left my shoulders to roam up and down my arms. "It's warm and comfortable, and so very *private*."

The smile I attempted wobbled. "I think we've seen all there is to see. I doubt I'll be able to sleep again before rehearsal. Perhaps we can go for a coffee? You can tell me more about my parents."

But Tomas seemed to have slipped into a place from which he couldn't withdraw. "Do you know what you mean to me?" The normally melodic voice cracked. He took my hand, lifting my fingers to his lips, and looked into my eyes as he kissed my knuckles. "I've been watching, keeping you safe. I followed you home one day."

167

My breath caught, and I cleared my throat, trying not to show my alarm. *He'd been in the SUV. Tomas, not Peters.*

"Why didn't you speak to me?"

"I didn't want you to know about me yet. I just wanted to watch you. Let you know someone cared. Then that man on the motorcycle arrived. The boyfriend you say you've gotten back with. He's not good enough for you, Morgan. He can't take care of you like I can."

Fear washed over me like ice water. How much did this man know about me? And here I was alone with him, somewhere no one would interrupt for hours. *So stupid.* I needed to get him to take me somewhere public.

Zeke. God, how I wished he were there.

"Maybe not," I said, playing along.

Tomas' eyes lit up behind his glasses. "You understand?"

"Yeah. I mean, he doesn't take care of me like... like you do." I looked away, unable to hold that disturbing gaze for long. "Seriously, let's go back to my place." Maybe I could get someone's attention on the way up to my apartment, or jump out of his car and run.

Tomas wasn't listening. "I want to always be everything you need, Morgan." He pulled me into a suffocating embrace, and it took everything I had not to struggle. I didn't want to see what happened when he got angry.

"I've had an exhausting day," I said against his shirt, tears leaking from my eyes in spite of myself. I began to shiver with fear.

"I know what's best for you, *mon ange*. You must do as I say." Tomas lifted my chin and kissed me again, this time pushing his tongue into my mouth. I curled my fist into his shirt, trying to keep him from getting any closer, nerves buzzing with anxiety.

"When you dance," he whispered breathlessly into my ear, "I'm transported." He attacked my throat with lips and tongue, shoving my coat from my shoulders, effectively trapping my arms with it. My heart pounded hard, adrenaline coursing through me.

"Tomas—"

"Call me *Daddy*, *mon petit*. I've longed for it."

What?

Hands on my ass, Tomas jerked my groin against his very aroused bulge. "Do it, Morgan. I want to hear the word from your lips."

My mind raced. I'd heard of a Daddy fetish, even seen it on porn sites, but this was something entirely different. Something unhealthy borne of obsession. Tomas had focused on me for years, his interest combining a need to nurture with sexual desire. All I could think was to mollify him enough he wouldn't become violent, and to do that I needed to play upon his need to take care of me.

"D-daddy," I managed. It wasn't difficult to sound frightened and unsure. "Please. I'm so tired. I want to go to bed."

A shudder ran through Tomas, and he lowered his hands from my back down my loose sweatpants to my ass, curling his fingers between the cheeks.

"I want that, too. So much," he said hoarsely.

Oh, God. God, no.

I became light-headed in his grasp. His lips latched onto my earlobe and sucked, breath hot and heavy in my ear.

"You want Daddy to tuck you in? You want Daddy's dick to suck on?" he whispered, and stark, cold, terror rocketed through me.

I pushed Tomas away, surprising him enough that he let go, and darted out of the room for the stairs, taking them two at a time until I reached the second landing. Tripping over my own feet, I righted myself and kept running, heading for the front door. I could hear his steps behind me, getting closer. I reached into my coat pocket for my cell phone as I threw the front door open. His hand shot out and slammed it just before his body crushed mine.

The day I'd met Zeke flashed in my mind. How I'd thought he'd been there, in Nikki's apartment, to hurt me. Now someone really did want to hurt me, and all I wanted was for Zeke to save me. But Zeke didn't know what was happening. He thought I was at home, in bed, where I should be. I should be. God, why had I come here?

I could feel Tomas' steely hard erection against the small of my back. There was no doubt in my mind he enjoyed my fear. Between my body and the door, I managed to maneuver my cell phone between the elastic of my sweatpants and the dip between my hip and stomach.

"Naughty, naughty boy," Tomas said in my ear. "Mustn't run from Daddy."

"I'm... I'm sorry." Nose pressed painfully to the door, the woodgrain blurred in front of my teary eyes.

"You're going to be even more sorry, *mon ange*. So much more sorry." Tomas reached around and palmed my crotch, just missing brushing against the bottom edge of my phone. He turned me and pushed me down to my knees.

Shaking, I looked up at him.

"My boy looks so pretty with his big eyes begging like that." Tomas grabbed me by the hair and pulled, forcing me to half-walk, half-crawl after him. In the next room, he ordered me to sit down.

Scalp smarting, I crouched near the wall, watching Tomas pace and mumble angrily to himself, his sophisticated veneer completely gone, replaced by something agitated and cruel. With trembling fingers, I reached for my phone. Slowly, I slid it out of my pants, concealing it as much as possible, and used my fingerprint to unlock the screen. I was thankful I always kept the volume setting on silent due to rehearsals.

"All Daddy wanted was a little cuddle, and what does my boy do? He runs," Tomas muttered to himself, continuing to pace.

Eyes flicking back and forth from the volatile man in front of me to my phone screen, I used one finger to open my contacts and scroll quickly to the bottom. The list was alphabetical, putting Zeke at the end. I pressed call, making sure to mute the sound. As soon as the screen indicated someone had picked up, I tucked the phone out of sight and said loudly, "Tomas, you have to let me go."

Tomas rounded on me, and I pressed my back against the wall in fear. *Zeke, please have heard that.*

"Naughty boys who run from their daddy are not permitted to speak!" Tomas barked. I opened my mouth to say something else, and he charged at me and smacked my face so hard, the opposite cheek hit the wall. More tears sprung to my eyes and rolled down my cheeks.

"Beautiful," Tomas breathed. "How beautiful your tears are to me, *mon beau*."

In a small voice, I said, "Daddy, please take me home. I don't like this place." I knew I needed to let Zeke know where we were, but I couldn't figure out a way to insert it without tipping off Tomas.

I flinched when Tomas touched my head, but he only carded his fingers gently through my hair. "I told you before, Daddy likes it here. And you have earned yourself a punishment."

170

I'd never been so scared in my life. I started praying to my dead brother. *Jake, are you up there? Please help me. Please get me out of this.* I itched to look at my phone hidden beneath my knee to make sure it was still connected but couldn't take the chance.

"T-this part of the Bronx is dangerous," I said. "And we shouldn't be here at the center."

"Daddy's with you. You don't have to be afraid." Tomas leaned toward me and pressed his lips to mine. "Kiss Daddy," he said roughly when I didn't respond.

I shut my eyes tightly and kissed him back. Tomas took me by the arm and helped me to my feet. Terrified he'd see my phone with its lit screen, I reached up and pulled his face down to mine again, kissing him harder while nudging the mobile behind me with my foot.

Tomas chuckled low in his throat, a sound that sent shivers down my spine. "That's a good boy. You want Daddy, don't you? Now, why don't we go back upstairs for your punishment and then have some fun?"

I allowed myself to be led out of the room, hoping against hope that Zeke had heard and would come. He knew about the LGBTQ center. I'd mentioned the Bronx. It would have to be enough. Belatedly, I realized I should have dialed 911. They could trace the call. But Zeke was the first person I'd thought of, the one person I wanted to see. He would phone the police.

God, I wished he was there. *Find me, Zeke.*

By continuing to eagerly kiss Tomas on our way up the stairs, I managed to slow our progress. *I deserve an academy award for this*, I thought, on the edge of getting hysterical.

I didn't know how I was keeping it together. Part of me wanted to start screaming until Tomas knocked me out, but what would he do to me then? My face hurt where he'd hit me, and my scalp still stung from the hair-pulling. His movements were becoming increasingly agitated, and I was afraid he was losing his grip on reality.

At the top of the stairs, Tomas dragged me into the nearest bedroom and shoved me down on the bed. He towered over me. He seemed to get off on my submission to him. If I could just get through this without things becoming sexual...

"Daddy." I held shaking arms up to him. "I need a hug."

"I don't know if you deserve hugs," Tomas said. "You ran from me before."

"I'm sorry. I'm sorry. Hold me. Please."

Tomas eased onto the bed beside me and gathered me into his arms. I clung to him. He smelled of expensive cologne. We both still wore coats, and he placed his hand beneath mine over my hammering heart. A slow smile that chilled me to the bone spread over his face.

Tremors ran through me, much like after a bad nightmare. I held onto him, concentrating on nothing but eating up time.

Tomas pried my hands from around his neck. "That's enough, now, Morgan. Time for your punishment."

"No," I whimpered, not faking my distress. *What the fuck was he going to do?*

"Over my knee, boy."

My eyes widened. Really? He was going to *spank* me? I listened hard, hoping to hear sirens, but only sounds of traffic filled the silence.

Tomas patted his knee, a frown on his face. "Don't you dare run away from me again, boy." His tone brooked no argument. Reluctantly, I started to lean over his lap.

"Take off your coat first."

With shaking hands, I removed my coat and placed it on the bed.

"Good boy. Now, over my knee."

I bent forward, balancing with my fingers on the floor, face very close to the bedstead. My gaze landed on something shiny on the wood just before Tomas slapped my buttocks, hard.

I let out a yell, and he did it again. And again. I was glad he hadn't told me to pull down my pants; the act was humiliating enough as it was, and God knew it hurt.

"You must never run from Daddy," Tomas said before smacking my ass a fifth time, then a sixth, getting harder with every blow. "If you do, the consequences will be worse." *Smack. Smack. Smack.*

God, I'm stuck in a nightmare. Somebody wake me up.

I lost count of how many times Tomas hit my ass, hand like iron. He held me down with an arm across my back and muttered about what a bad boy I'd been to run from him, and how I deserved a red backside for my disobedience.

When he finished, I was sobbing, my ass sore in spite of the layer of clothes between it and his hand, and my pride crumpled.

Behind the beating of my heart, my sniffles, and Tomas' heavy breathing, I heard sirens. I was sure of it this time. Tomas appeared unaware, even after the red and blue lights flashed into the windows.

"Are you sorry you were bad for Daddy?" Tomas asked, allowing me to rest on my knees and cupping my face in his hands. He kissed me, licking the tears off my cheeks until I jerked away. I heard the door downstairs open and stumbled to my feet and ran from him for the second time that night.

When I bolted down the stairs, two guns swung toward me. I heard Zeke yell something and then I was in his arms, legs wrapped around his middle, police officers clomping up the steps behind me.

Zeke held me tightly, face pressed against the side of my head. "God, Morgan. God," he kept repeating.

"I'm sorry," I sobbed, not even sure what I was sorry for, exactly.

The police officers appeared on the stairs with Tomas docile and handcuffed between them. His eyes immediately sought me out.

"You ran again, Morgan," he said.

"You're a fucking lunatic!" Zeke yelled at him, shielding me with his body as the officers led Tomas past us.

"You'll need to bring him to the precinct," one of them said. I squeezed my eyes shut again.

CHAPTER TWENTY-TWO

Epilogue Zeke

I'd never been so scared as I had been when I'd gotten the call from Morgan and heard that psychopath in the background. If Blaze hadn't been around, I don't know if I would have had the presence of mind to be able to get help as fast as I did. He'd called the police while I kept listening on the phone and freaking the hell out when I couldn't hear Morgan anymore, wondering what the fuck that sonovabitch Marchant was doing to him. When Morgan had mentioned the Bronx and then the center, I'd remembered the LGBTQ center, and Blaze and I had jumped on our bikes, arriving just behind the police. The terror of seeing them raise their guns at Morgan rode on the heels of my sheer relief that he was alive.

Thank God Marchant hadn't had time to sexually assault Morgan, although what he had done had been traumatizing enough. Along with going psycho and scaring the shit out of him, I found out the creep had turned Morgan over his knee and *spanked* him, for Christ's sake. When I'd seen the bruising on Morgan's ass, I'd wanted to kill the fucker.

Marchant was charged with false imprisonment, assault, and battery, but let's be real: his money would keep him from seeing much jail time. I at least hoped the bad publicity would put a significant hole in his wallet. Yeah, I'd made sure the story leaked to a friend of the club's connected with the press, keeping Morgan's name carefully out of it, of course.

After visiting the station and giving a statement, I held Morgan all night in his bed, swearing to God and anyone else who would listen that I'd never leave his side again.

The following Saturday after Marchant's arrest, we stopped by the opening of the LGBTQ center before going out to lunch. Morgan had been wary about returning there but insisted on facing his fears. Besides, he said there was something he wanted to look at. I'll admit, I was curious about what it could be.

"It'll only take a minute," he said. Muted voices rose from the crowd of people gathered in the room behind the kitchen where all the food was set up. Balloons in all colors floated about the ceiling. Morgan led me up the stairs to the second floor.

I squeezed his hand, which was trembling a little. "You sure you want to come up here?"

"I need to see something." Morgan switched on the light in one of the rooms. "This is where we were," he said, moving slowly toward the bed.

I followed.

Crouching, Morgan lifted the blue bedspread and peered at the wooden bed frame.

"What is it?" I asked.

"When Tomas was..." Morgan hesitated, "Well, I saw this." He showed me something on the oak wood of the bed.

"What's is it?" I asked.

"Just what I thought. This bed came from Easter Furniture," Morgan said.

"Does that mean something?"

"Gabe told me all the furniture for the center was donated from local stores, which means Albert Easter donated this bed. According to Gerald Peters, Easter was furious about having an LGBTQ center near his store. So, why would he donate furniture to it?"

I raised my brows and shrugged, unsure of what Morgan was getting at.

He got to his feet. "I think Gerald Peters lied. He's been stirring up trouble, and I'm going to get to the bottom of it. Whoever's responsible for the threatening notes—and I suspect it's only Gerald—is going to be out of Wentworth Properties."

"Good for you," I said, gathering him into my arms. God, he felt amazing there. I'd been crazy to ever have pushed him away.

"I wish you'd told me about the notes," I said into his hair.

"I wasn't really worried about them," he said. "Besides, you and I weren't exactly talking."

"I would have come if you'd needed me," I swore, wanting to kick myself for staying away.

Morgan smiled. "I know. Marchant's admitted to being behind the hang up calls and heavy breathing."

Before I could say anything about that, Morgan continued, "Your dad still meeting us for lunch?"

"I invited him, but I can't guarantee he'll be there."

"And you're okay with it if he doesn't show?"

I squeezed the back of Morgan's neck and kissed the side of his head. "Perfectly fine with it."

Morgan looked dubious. "But he's your dad."

I shook him gently by the scruff. "You're the most important person in my life."

"I'm proud of you for telling him."

I tilted up Morgan's chin with my finger and looked into his dark eyes. "I didn't run from you because I was ashamed, you know. It was..."

"You were scared and insecure."

I made a face. I wasn't exactly proud of it, especially since what I'd done had made it possible for Marchant to get closer to Morgan. "Yeah."

"But now you realize you're more than good enough for me."

"I'll never be good enough for you."

Morgan ruffled. "That's not true!"

I smiled. "Doesn't matter. I've realized nothing's worth losing you." I leaned in and kissed him. Belatedly, I wondered if kissing him in the room where Marchant had done the same was such a good idea, but Morgan leaned into me and kissed me right back. I wanted to erase every touch the man had laid on Morgan, but that would have to wait.

Downstairs, we said our goodbyes to Gabe, Jon, and the others before climbing on my bike. I'd bought a helmet for Morgan. I liked the feel of his arms wrapped around me and his chest pressed against my back as we rode, and he said he liked being my *biker bitch*, the idiot. It didn't go unnoticed he got hard when riding with me.

When we'd made it to the small family restaurant and ordered, I could tell something was on Morgan's mind.

"Why're you frowning like that?" I asked.

"I was just thinking about Jake," Morgan said.

"What about him?"

"Do you really think he had something going with that girl? It just doesn't seem like him to be with someone who's cheating."

I rubbed the whiskers on my chin. "Blaze and I have wondered the same thing. Vanessa could've been on his bike for some other reason, I guess. Who knows?"

Morgan nodded and was silent a moment before a little smile tugged at his lips. "I've got some news."

"Yeah?"

Morgan fiddled with his napkin. "I've told Mr. Brainard I don't want to continue my apprenticeship. After the final performance of *Cinderella*, I'm done."

I stared at him a long moment, the words sinking in. "What? But, how come? I mean, I know you've been through a lot, but he said he'd give you some time—"

"Yeah, he did," Morgan interrupted. "And I appreciate it. But I've decided devoting myself to ballet isn't what I want anymore. The thought's been at the back of my mind a while now, but it took what happened with Tomas to force me to make the decision. A career in ballet doesn't leave me any time for anything else. Not for you, not for my friends, not for my company, not for volunteer work. I have absolutely no leisure time, and I don't want that life anymore."

"So, you're giving it up? Your dream?"

Morgan shook his head. "My dream's changed. I still want to dance; I'm just not joining a company or aiming to be a principal dancer. I'm going to instruct at the school instead." He smiled, and he looked happy. "I'm also going to teach a ballet class at the center."

The thought of having more time with Morgan put a big smile on my face. "If that's what you want."

He nodded. "It is. It was a difficult decision, but now that I've made it, I feel so relieved."

"I'm definitely all for you having more time to be with me."

"I thought you would be." Morgan gave me a smug look.

Our food came, and we ate, grinning at each other and touching our knees together under the table. Pop didn't show. Not like I was expecting him to; that kind of thing only happened in books or movies. I'd thrown the invite out there, and he hadn't taken me up on it. That was okay. Maybe someday it wouldn't be okay anymore, and if that happened, I'd decide what I wanted to do then. Or maybe

Pop would come around. Who knew? Thing was, I just didn't give a damn what my old man thought of me. And that felt good.

I hadn't been lying when I'd told Morgan I wasn't good enough for him, but I had to admit if a swanky guy like Tomas Marchant could turn out to be such a creep, maybe I needed to adjust the way I judged people. Morgan had been quick to assure me that, Marchant aside, a person having a "daddy kink" was neither all that uncommon nor anything to be ashamed of. He might be right about that, but Marchant definitely took it to a twisted level. If we never saw his face again, it would be too soon.

Later that night, after I pounded Morgan in the shower until both our legs turned to jelly, we lay side by side in Morgan's bed, sated and sleepy. I decided it was a good time to bring up the subject that had been stewing in my mind ever since Nikki had paid me that visit.

"Hey," I took Morgan's hand and kissed it. "Were you a virgin the first time we were together?"

Morgan avoided my gaze. "I told you Nikki was my first."

I lowered my voice to a growl. "You know what I mean."

He glanced at me. "I didn't think you could tell."

"I couldn't. Morgan, thank God I took my time with you!"

Morgan sat up, covers pooling in his lap. "How'd you know, then?" I watched the truth dawn on him. "I'm going to kill Nikki."

"She was just looking out for you. I don't blame her for being pissed. I was being a jerk."

"You didn't know. It's not like you purposely took my virginity and dumped me."

"It looked that way to her. And I didn't dump you."

Morgan crossed his arms over his bare chest. "You were considering it."

I tugged the sheet down to his knees and pressed a kiss to the inside of his thigh, loving the way he trembled at the touch of my lips to his skin.

"Naw. Every time I thought about it, I felt like barfing," I murmured before tonguing the crease between Morgan's leg and groin.

"How romantic."

I chuckled before pressing a kiss higher up. "Can't stay away from you long. Never thought I'd wanna spend the rest of my life with a guy."

Morgan tensed. Grasping my hair with his fingers, he lifted my head so I was looking at his face. "You want to spend the rest of your life with me?"

"No, I was talkin' about Ax." I rolled my eyes. "Of course, you, dummy."

Morgan pounced on me, rolling me onto my back. "Me, too. With you." He grinned so big I could see all his teeth and then the next second he became deadly serious. "I love you."

My breath caught in my throat. What this kid did to me. "Yeah." I swallowed. "Me, too."

The grin returned. "Move in with me."

I gave a beleaguered sigh. "Guess it wouldn't be much of a hardship to wake up to your face every morning — ouch! No pinching!" I tucked him up under my arm and spread the sheet over us. "I might even let you get me into a monkey suit and take me to one of those cheese tasting things sometime."

Morgan leaned his head back to look up at me. "A cheese tasting thing?"

"Yeah, you know, don't you fancy guys go to those?"

Morgan snorted and pinched my side again, harder this time, and it was my turn to wrestle him onto his back. "You're gonna pay for that, tiny dancer."

"I hope so."

I started singing the Elton John song by the same name as I pressed kisses to Morgan's shoulders and chest as his stomach quivered beneath my hand. I'd meant what I'd said; I'd dress up any way and do anything Morgan wanted me to as long as I could keep him smiling that smile.

Mostly, I just wanted to make sure Morgan knew he wasn't alone anymore. He had me, and I wasn't going anywhere. He could take that to the bank.

THE END

Thank you for reading *The Ballerino and the Biker*, the first book in my *Hedonist* MC series. Please check out my other works, including *The River Wolf Pack* series, which includes hot wolf shifters, m-preg, and a bit of political intrigue between humans and werewolves.

Subscribe to my newsletter for freebies and release announcements. I rarely send out more than one a month.

https://madmimi.com/signups

If you enjoy sci-fantasy, I currently have two full-length novels in that genre, The Wolves of Daos 5 and Teresias Bound. You can see my books and read blurbs and reviews on my Amazon page:

https://www.amazon.com/RebeccaJames/e/B017OG2OQ0/

Happy reading!

My website:

https://rebeccajamesgayromance.wordpress.com/

About the Author

Rebecca James majored in English literature. She is married and has three children. She loves animals, books, and family.

BOOKS BY REBECCA JAMES

Contemporary

The Hedonist Series

- The Ballerino and the Biker

Paranormal

The River Wolf Pack Series

- First Omega
- Second Alpha
- Third Mate

The Angel Hills Series

- Omega Arrival
- Ripples of Threat

The Cascade City Pack Series

- A New Beginning
- Breaking the Bonds

Sci-fantasy

- The Wolves of Daos 5
- Teresias Bound

Novellas

- Love Lost, Love Found
- Love Will Find a Way

Made in United States
North Haven, CT
24 March 2022

17490245R00114